"I Can See Why You Like Living Here. It's Very Comfortable, Very Real..."

Trent's voice trailed off as he stopped talking, afraid that he might have said too much.

"Very real—that's an odd thing to say. Where do you come from, Trent? Where have you lived that wasn't real?"

"I was referring to the people as much as the place. Real people without pretenses. Even Mike—he doesn't like me and he makes no effort to hide the fact. I much prefer that to someone who smiles at my face while twisting the knife in my back."

Cassie swallowed the last sip of her wine and set the glass on the window ledge next to the swing. She turned to face him, studying his handsome features in the silvery moonlight. "Who are you, Trent Nichols?" Her gaze held his, her eyes searching for his hidden truth.

"I'm...I don't know. I used to know, but I don't anymore. Somewhere along the way I seem to have lost myself."

Dear Reader,

This month we have a very special treat in store for you. It's the Silhouette Desire "Premiere" author for 1993! This is a completely new, never-before-published writer, who we have chosen as someone exciting and outstanding. Her name is Carol Devine, and her book is *Beauty and the Beastmaster*. There is a letter in it from her to all of you, her new fans. *Who* is the Beauty and just who—or what—is the Beastmaster? Well, I'm not telling; you'll have to read and find out.

In addition to our "Premiere" author, October has five more favorites. Our *Man of the Month* is from the delightful Cait London. The lineup is completed with wonderful books by Jackie Merritt, Christine Rimmer, Noelle Berry McCue and Shawna Delacorte.

As for *next* month... it's a winner! We've decided to "Heat Up Your Winter" with six of our most sensuous, most spectacular authors: Ann Major, Dixie Browning, Barbara Boswell, Robin Elliott, Mary Lynn Baxter and Lass Small. Silhouette Desire... you just can't get *any* better than this.

All the best,

Lucia Macro
Senior Editor

SHAWNA DELACORTE

CASSIE'S LAST GOODBYE

SILHOUETTE *Desire*®

™ Published by Silhouette Books New York

America's Publisher of Contemporary Romance

SILHOUETTE BOOKS
300 East 42nd St., New York, N.Y. 10017

CASSIE'S LAST GOODBYE

Copyright © 1993 by Sharon K. Dennison

ISBN: 0-373-05814-4

First Silhouette Books printing October 1993

All the characters in this book have no existence outside the imagination of the author and have no relation whatsoever to anyone bearing the same name or names. They are not even distantly inspired by any individual known or unknown to the author, and all incidents are pure invention.

® and ™:Trademarks used with authorization. Trademarks indicated with ® are registered in the United States Patent and Trademark Office, the Canada Trade Mark Office and in other countries.

Printed in the U.S.A.

Books by Shawna Delacorte

Silhouette Desire

Sarah and the Stranger #730
The Bargain Bachelor #759
Cassie's Last Goodbye #814

SHAWNA DELACORTE

lives in Southern California, where she has worked for several years in television production. She has always enjoyed writing, but it was not until she switched from nonfiction to fiction that she felt she had found a happy home.

An avid photographer who loves to travel, Shawna laughs as she says, "You should see me getting on a plane—my laptop computer hanging from one shoulder, my camera bag hanging from the other and my purse somewhere in between. Sometimes I actually have to hold my boarding pass with my teeth."

One

"**C**assie, honey. Could I have a refill?" The ruddy-faced fisherman in his late fifties held up his cup. She immediately grabbed the coffee and filled the empty mug.

"You're in luck, Jake." She flashed him a warm, open smile. "It's a freshly brewed pot." It was a typical early breakfast—locals, no tourists. The atmosphere was noisy, open and friendly. Everyone knew everyone and no one had any secrets. It still amazed her when she thought of how easily she had adapted to the life-style on the island and how quickly the locals had accepted an outsider.

It was strange how fate worked. One year ago she was in Chicago—a divorce having just been granted following a year of bitter arguments and legal battles—with a job as the youngest promoted woman vice president at a large banking concern and a borderline case of burnout. All of that at the age of thirty-two. Then the letter came. She had been named as sole heir to her aunt Sofie's estate. She was surprised to find that she had inherited a small restaurant and bar on one of the San Juan Islands in the channel just off the Washington mainland.

"I don't know what you do to the coffee—" Jake's robust laugh filled the air "—but it's quite an improvement over what Sofie used to serve."

She reached across the counter and gave a friendly pat to his potbelly. "You old teddy bear, flattery like that will not get you a free breakfast, so just stop trying." She dearly adored Jake. From her first day on the island he had taken her under his wing, helped her acclimatize and fit in with her new surroundings. He had been a father figure in her time of need.

Jake drained the last of the coffee from his cup and tossed some money on the counter. "I'll see you later." He left the restaurant, pausing to exchange a few words with almost everyone there.

The next two hours continued to be very busy, with a constant stream of customers—all hungry. Finally everything settled down, the last customer of the morning having just left. She took advantage of the lull to restock some supplies and get ready for the lunch crowd. "Anne, now would be a good time for you and Danny to run to the store. We're running short on several items."

The plump woman in her early fifties with the warm, open face wiped her hands on her apron as she walked in from the kitchen. Her tone was cheery and upbeat. "Whew! That was quite a breakfast rush. For a while there I had the entire grill covered with eggs, bacon, sausage, hash browns and had three omelets working all at the same time." Anne offered a good-natured laugh. "I was about ready to call for a time-out. If it hadn't been for Danny giving me a hand you'd still have customers waiting for food. It was like everyone in town decided to eat breakfast here instead of at home."

Cassie looked around the restaurant. "Where's Danny now?" She peered through the door leading to the kitchen.

"He finally caught up with the dishes and now he's taking out the trash." Anne paused for a moment, her brow furrowed in thought. "If I take Danny with me, you'll be here all alone. We'll probably be gone for at least half an hour."

"I'll be just fine. Mike should be here in fifteen minutes to start setting up the bar before lunch. If I run into a sudden rush of last-minute breakfast customers he can give me a hand."

Anne untied her apron and laid it aside. "We'll be back as soon as we can." She hurried through the kitchen and out the back door.

Trent Nichols walked up the ramp from the dock to the main street of the small harbor town. He had not planned to make this particular stop but had promised to do a favor for a friend, a Seattle attorney by the name of Randall Davies. Randall had received a letter from a man who said he had recently inherited a large parcel of land, including a motel, with a restaurant and bar next door. There was also a house behind the restaurant.

Randall had never met the man nor seen the property, and was not sure exactly why this man, Bob Hampton, had contacted him rather than using the attorney who would have been involved in the inheritance. Bob Hampton had asked Randall to represent him but did not say exactly why he was seeking his representation or what he was trying to accomplish. The letter was disturbingly vague. His first inclination was to dismiss the letter and refuse to accept this potential client. But since Trent was headed in that direction, anyway, Randall had asked his friend to do him a favor and check out the situation for him.

Trent approached the motel and was immediately surprised to find a Closed sign on the door. That was very odd. It was May and even if the motel was only seasonal it should now be open for the summer season. He did a quick, superficial inspection of the outside of the motel buildings. They were in need of repair, but it appeared to be primarily cosmetic refurbishing. He could also see where expanding, updating the facilities and adding more resort amenities, such as a spa and pool, would be in order. There seemed to be plenty of vacant land available; he assumed the surrounding land belonged with the motel. Hopefully, he would be able to get a look inside.

It again struck him as odd. The prime location and the fact that there was no discernible competition in the immediate area indicated that it should be a profitable operation, one that could sustain a year-round clientele. He glanced next door toward the restaurant, which appeared to be open. Perhaps someone there could tell him where he could locate the new owner of the property.

Cassie continued to fill saltshakers, sugar jars, cream pitchers and napkin holders. Before she could finish, she ran out of napkins. She searched the cartons on the floor of the storeroom but none of them contained the supply of napkins. Then the sought-after carton caught her eye. It was on the top shelf in the hallway.

She grabbed the rickety old wooden stepladder and placed it below the shelf. Steadying herself with one hand against the wall, she climbed up four steps. She berated herself for not listening to Mike and buying a new ladder. She cautiously reached for the carton. Hearing the front door of the restaurant open and close she called out, "Is that you, Mike? I could sure use some help."

Cassie, a petite five foot three if she stretched it, was not quite tall enough to reach the carton. She tentatively climbed one more step to the top of the ladder. With both arms stretched above her head she tried to coax the box off the shelf with her fingertips. The unstable ladder finally reached its limits. It began to sway.

She reached out, desperately trying to grab on to something—anything that would keep her from falling. She felt the ladder slip out from under her as she tumbled backward, out of control. Then Cassie felt herself being caught in a pair of strong arms and heard the smooth tone of an unfamiliar male voice.

"Mike isn't here. Will I do?"

She instinctively clung to her rescuer, wrapping her arms around his neck. A quick intake of breath was her immediate response as she turned her head and looked up into sky blue eyes that twinkled with amusement. She instantly became aware of his taut, muscular body and tanned good looks.

"What's going on here?" She turned toward the sound of the familiar voice belonging to the stocky, fifty-five-year-old bartender standing in the doorway. "Cassie, are you all right?"

She quickly regained her composure. "I'm fine, Mike, thanks to this gentleman. He caught me in the nick of time—just before I would have hit the floor." She was very aware that he had made no effort to put her down. His smile mesmerized her, sending unexpected little tremors through her being.

With a flush of embarrassment covering her cheeks, she lowered her eyelids. Her voice held a hint of shyness. "I . . . I believe you can put me down now."

"Oh, yeah." His tone of voice teased her as he carried her out into the restaurant and set her on a counter stool. "You're such a tiny thing I didn't realize I was still holding you."

Mike's expression was cautious as he carefully eyed the stranger. "Are you sure everything's okay here, Cassie?"

"Everything's fine, Mike. Go on and set up the bar."

He still seemed reticent about leaving her alone with the stranger. He looked toward the kitchen. "Where are Anne and Danny?"

"They're shopping. We had such a rush of business this morning that we were close to being out of some items, so I thought it would be wise if we stocked up during the lull before lunch."

Mike shot one last look at the stranger, then turned toward the swinging doors that separated the bar from the restaurant. "I'll be right here if you need me." He disappeared into the other room and they soon heard the sounds of bottles and glasses being readied for business.

Cassie turned her attention toward the stranger. "Thanks for coming to my rescue. I'd hate to think of what might have happened if you hadn't been there." She smiled warmly and extended her hand. "I'm Cassie Brockton."

He grasped the warmth of her hand in his and returned her smile. "Trent Nichols. It was my pleasure. Rescuing damsels in distress is my forte."

She took a moment to carefully look him over. He was even better looking than she had first thought. He stood about five feet eleven inches tall and had a youthful appearance despite the little wrinkles she could see at the corners of his eyes and the beginnings of a furrow to his brow. His blond hair was shaggy and needed cutting, but she could tell it had once been a very stylish haircut. She guessed his age to be about forty, maybe a little younger.

He appeared to be personally well-groomed in spite of his hair, and even though his jeans were frayed and the sweatshirt he wore had ragged edges where the sleeves had been cut off, they were clean. "I've never seen you before. Are you new on the island?"

"Yes, I just arrived."

She glanced out the window and saw the ferryboat pulling away from the dock. "So I see."

Her statement confused him until he turned and followed her line of sight to the ferryboat. He started to correct her but then caught himself and allowed her incorrect assumption to stand. Discretion was in order until he had time to assess the situation. Randall had not yet accepted Bob Hampton as a client, so the less said, the better. "This was the first restaurant I saw, so here I am."

Cassie jumped up and hurried behind the counter. "You're probably wanting some coffee." She grabbed the pot and looked at the remaining coffee, then quickly set it aside. Grabbing a clean pot, she shoved it into the machine and pressed the button. "That stuff's pretty old. In fact, it's so strong that it could probably serve itself. I'll have a fresh pot in a couple of minutes. Meanwhile—" she grabbed a menu and handed it to him "—you can look over the selections."

He took the menu from her. "I was just next door, at the motel—" He saw an expression of anger dart across her face as her hazel eyes darkened and narrowed.

"I'm sorry if Bob Hampton has misled you." Her words were clipped and her voice held an edge to it. The sudden change in her demeanor caught him completely off guard. "This restaurant is a separate business from the motel. There are no provisions for his guests being able to charge meals here and pay for them at the motel when they check out. I hope this doesn't inconvenience you."

He threw his hands up in a defensive mode, his face registering his surprise at her verbal attack. "Whoa! Back off. I was only going to say that I had just been next door and was surprised to find the motel closed." He studied her reaction to his words, saw the blush come to her face.

She felt the embarrassment color her cheeks. Bob Hampton had been such a thorn in her side ever since his mother died and he had inherited everything. "I'm sorry. It's just that . . . well, I obviously made an erroneous assumption. Please accept my apology." She offered him an apologetic smile.

"No harm done." His smile and tone may have said that the matter was forgotten but that was far from the truth. There was more going on here than Randall Davies had been led to believe. The situation required more investigation than either he or Randall had originally thought. It appeared that if he was going to accurately evaluate the situation, he would need to stick around for a while, at least until he could talk to Bob Hampton and get the confusion straightened out.

She went to the back counter to get a coffee mug, a glass of water and a place setting. As she picked up the necessary items and filled the water glass she watched him in the mirror. He opened the menu and started to read it, then a look of concern quickly darted across his face. He put down the menu and reached into his pocket, withdrawing only a handful of change, no bills. He was obviously perturbed as he shoved the change back into his pocket and closed the menu.

Trent was, indeed, perturbed. He had left his wallet in the cabin of his boat. He had made the decision to allow her to think he had arrived on the ferry, and he did not want to create any suspicions until he had control of the situation. The ferry seemed less "outsider" than to admit he had arrived on his own boat—actually, a forty-five-foot power yacht that could sleep four people. Oh, well, he was not that hungry, anyway. He had only stopped at the harbor to carry out the promised favor for Randall, a business situation in which he had no personal interest. He had originally thought it would take only an hour or two of his time.

Trent studied the delightful young woman who had fallen so unexpectedly into his arms. Her petite size and short hair had, at first, made her seem more cute than anything else. As he looked at her more closely he realized she was much more than that. He took in the way her jeans hugged her hips and legs, accentuating a delightfully rounded bottom. Her sunny yellow blouse was neither low cut nor too tight, but it did manage to convey some rather enticing curves. Her bright hazel eyes sparkled when she talked and her finely sculpted features created a truly lovely face. She was definitely more than merely cute.

Cassie saw him close the menu. She returned and placed the coffee mug, glass of water and silverware in front of him. The pot was now filled with freshly brewed coffee. She grabbed it and filled his mug. "What would you like to eat?" She waited for his order.

"Nothing to eat, thanks. Just the coffee will be fine." He took a sip. "Good and hot," he said, then offered her a dazzling but sincere smile.

It was so obvious to Cassie. His worn clothes, his need of a haircut, the way he checked his money then closed the menu—he could not afford to buy breakfast. She appreciated and respected the fact that he did not try to con her out of a meal, did not eat then suddenly discover he had left his wallet in his other pants, did not even make mention of the fact that she certainly owed him something for saving her neck.

She projected an outgoing, teasing attitude, not wanting to embarrass him—at least, not any more than she probably already had with her unwarranted comment about his staying at the motel. "That will never do. If it weren't for you I'd surely have broken something, possibly several somethings. The very least I can do is show my appreciation by treating you to breakfast. Now, how do you like your eggs?"

Her smile was captivating, and he found her utterly enchanting. Perhaps this little town would be a good place for him to stay for a while after taking care of his business commitment to Randall. After all, he had had no particular plan or itinerary in mind when he had wrapped up all his own pressing business matters and told his partner he was taking off for about three months.

He needed to get his head together, to get away from the rat race. The stress and pressure associated with his high-profile Beverly Hills law firm had gotten to him. He needed a change of pace and scenery. He desperately needed to simplify his life.

Upon graduating top of his class from law school he had set a goal of being independently wealthy by the time he was forty. Through hard work and shrewd investments, coupled with a little bit of luck, he had completed that goal, still six months from that fortieth birthday. He did have to admit that some of his investment deals had been handled in a slightly underhanded manner —nothing illegal, just not as completely above-board as they might have been.

Now, however, it seemed he no longer had any purpose to his life; his work no longer excited him the way it used to. The public social whirl had also become more of a burden than a pleasure. He was tired of the endless string of status-seeking women. He wanted to settle down with someone real, someone who had her feet firmly planted in reality.

He returned his thoughts to her question. "I couldn't possibly allow you to cover the cost of my breakfast." He felt a little sheepish as he started to say he did not have his wallet on him at the moment but could certainly afford to pay for his meal.

She lowered her voice slightly and leaned toward him even though there was no one around to hear what she was going to say. "Look, I saw you check your money then decide not to order. I really do owe you for saving me from that fall. Now, I won't hear any more about it. If you don't tell me what you want, I'll just have to guess."

Perhaps he had become jaded over the years but the concept of lending a helping hand to your fellow man out of the goodness of your heart was something he had not come across in a long time. He glanced down at the way he was dressed—old, worn clothes and no money in his pockets. He could certainly understand why she would have made the assumption she did. He was finding Cassie Brockton more and more intriguing with each passing minute.

She liked his response. Not only did he not try to con her out of a meal, he had objected to the idea of her providing him with a free breakfast. He was articulate, and his blue eyes sparkled with intelligence. He clearly was a man who had simply run into some bad luck but still felt he should pay his own way and not accept any handouts, she thought. "How about the specialty of the house—fresh salmon steak, eggs, shepherd's potatoes, fruit compote and freshly squeezed orange juice."

"Sounds like a complete banquet...and I insist on paying for my breakfast." He took another sip of his coffee as he watched her hurry off toward the kitchen. He would pay her for his breakfast as soon as he retrieved his wallet from the boat. Meanwhile, he would kick back, relax and enjoy his conversation with Cassie.

Trent looked around, his practiced gaze taking in everything with a quick sweep of the room. It seemed to be a nice little operation, a restaurant with a separate bar. He wondered exactly how Cassie fit in. She apparently had the authority to offer him a free meal and Mike had deferred to her instructions to get to work.

She returned from the kitchen with a big glass of orange juice. "Anne should be back in no more than ten minutes, so if you can wait, you'll get a much more enjoyable breakfast than if I cook it myself."

His eyes twinkled as he teased her. "Not much of a hand in the kitchen, huh? Your husband have any problems with that?" His smile faded as he saw the quick look of anger flash through her eyes, followed closely by a look of resignation and a sigh.

"Not anymore, he doesn't." Her voice held a slight edge to it, different from the note he had detected when he had mentioned being at the motel. He saw the muscles in her jaw clench into a taut line.

"Hey, I'm sorry. I didn't mean to pry." He leveled a quizzical look at her.

Her face relaxed as she offered him a smile. "Don't worry about it—it's ancient history. He was a hotshot attorney who considered his exalted career far more important than my lowly career in banking." She refilled his coffee cup as she quickly changed the subject. "What brings you to the island?"

"Oh, just wandering around, looking for a nice place to light." He had caught the decidedly sharp edge of bitterness in her voice when she had mentioned "attorney." What should have been an easygoing and open conversation was becoming more and more complicated. He sensed there was definitely some sort of conflict between the motel and the restaurant. Bob Hampton's letter had alluded to the fact that he owned it all, but Cassie had emphatically stated that the restaurant was a separate business. And then, on top of that, this delightful young woman had very clearly voiced a decidedly low opinion of attorneys. "What about you? You lived here long?"

"No, not at all. Up until a year ago I lived in Chicago, then I inherited this place from my aunt and thought I'd try my hand at running it. Things were a little shaky for the first couple of months, but now I feel very comfortable and at home."

"This must have been quite an adjustment from Chicago." He was confused. Bob Hampton claimed to have inherited the property six months ago and now Cassie said she had inherited this business a year ago. Exactly who owned what?

She laughed, an open, warm laugh. He liked the way her nose crinkled up and her eyes sparkled. "You bet it was.'' She cleared away his empty orange juice glass, refilled his coffee cup, then ducked into the kitchen at the sound of the back door. She quickly returned. ''Anne is back. She'll have your food ready right away.''

A tall, gangly teenage boy of about eighteen appeared from the kitchen, carrying a sack from the store. He went immediately behind the counter and began putting things away.

Cassie turned toward him. ''Danny, could you please finish filling the napkin holders? I got distracted and didn't get it done.'' She started to turn her attention once again to Trent, then turned back to Danny. ''And put 'new stepladder' on the shopping list.''

Trent laughed. ''I'd say you certainly do need a new one.'' He was enjoying the conversation with Cassie.

''Well, enough about my carelessness.'' She felt a flush of embarrassment cover her cheeks as she recalled being cradled in his arms. She searched for something to change the subject. ''Are you planning to stay on the island for a while?''

''When I arrived I hadn't planned on staying, but . . .'' For the first time he searched the depths of her eyes as if trying to find answers to questions too long left unasked, solutions to problems too long left unresolved. ''I think I might like to stay for a while.'' It was a decision made independently of his need to tend to business for Randall. ''However, the motel seems to be closed. Is there somewhere close by where I could get a room?'' Again he was torn between his business necessities and his personal needs. He felt it would be better not to mention his boat, especially since he had already allowed the impression that he had arrived on the ferry.

Unexpected little tremors once again tried to well up inside her when her gaze locked with his. She felt the pull of his magnetism, almost a mystical meshing of their souls. Her voice was less than firm. "I, uh, I have a room that I sometimes rent out during the summer tourist season. It has its own entrance to the outside and a private bathroom. It's reasonably priced..." She felt the embarrassment rise on her cheeks as she looked into his clear blue eyes. "If you'd be interested."

Two

Trent jumped at the unexpected turn of events. It would be a perfect situation. He would be able to gather the information Randall needed without arousing unnecessary suspicions about his presence.

With each passing minute he was becoming more and more captivated by Cassie—a personal interest totally separate from any business considerations for Randall Davies. Yes, indeed. This little town on this island just might be the ideal place to spend a few weeks away from everything.

Trent told Cassie that his belongings were stored down at the dock. He would get them and return right away. As soon as he finished breakfast he left the restaurant, hurried to his boat and packed what he would need for two weeks. He toyed with the idea of staying the entire summer.

He felt uncomfortable about deceiving Cassie this way, but he convinced himself that it was a harmless deception, especially in light of her adverse opinion of the legal profession. No one would be hurt by it. He would take care of business as quickly as possible, leaving the rest of his time free to relax and indulge the simple joys of everyday life.

He might even check into buying a summer place on the island.

Cassie, meanwhile, informed Mike, Anne and Danny that she had rented her spare room to Trent. Anne and Danny seemed surprised, but Mike, on the other hand, was decidedly hostile toward the idea. Trent Nichols was a stranger, an outsider. Mike did not trust outsiders. Actually, Mike did not trust much of anyone.

It had taken Jake to convince Mike that Cassie was okay and could be trusted. Now, however, he felt as protective of her as Jake did. He could not stop her from renting a room in her house to this outsider, but he could keep an eye on him to make sure everything was all right—make sure this Trent Nichols was not taking advantage of Cassie's open, giving nature.

Trent returned to the restaurant with his suitcase. After introductions were made, Cassie turned toward Mike. "If you could keep an eye on things I'll get Trent settled into his room then be right back."

"Sure thing, Cassie." Mike shot a look of warning toward Trent as he watched him follow her out the door. As soon as they were out of sight Mike turned to Anne. "She doesn't know a thing about this guy. He just wandered in from the ferryboat and she decided to rent him a room." Mike looked in the direction Trent and Cassie had gone, then returned his attention to Anne. "I can tell you one thing. I'm going to be keeping my eye on this guy. She's just too trusting.''

Anne laughed at Mike's skepticism. Both were life-long residents of the island and had known each other forever. The same with Jake. When Anne's husband had died both Mike and Jake had been there to help her through the rough times. It was Jake who, five years ago, had talked her into doing the cooking for Sofie—a happy situation for all concerned, since Anne was an excellent cook and her presence greatly increased business. And it was obvious to everyone who knew them that Jake, a lifelong bachelor, had a real schoolboy type of crush on Anne.

"Honestly, Mike. I think you'd be suspicious of the good Lord himself.''

He allowed a frown to crease his brow, a crease hardly noticeable among all the others in his weathered face. ''Not if he had proper identification.''

"Cassie knows what she's doing. I'm sure she learned to be a real good judge of character living in a big city like Chicago and being in charge of that bank.''

"Yeah, well . . . maybe so, but I'm keeping my eye on this guy just the same. Something's not right about him.''

Suitcase in hand, Trent followed Cassie up the path to the old two-story house that sat up above the restaurant looking out over the harbor and to the islands beyond. There was a large covered porch with an old-fashioned swing. Pots of brightly colored flowers were placed along the porch railing. She opened the screen door and went inside. He followed. ''This is the living room. Across the hall—'' she indicated with a wave of her hand ''—is the dining room.'' She continued past the staircase toward the back of the house. ''Down this way is the kitchen.''

He followed her down the hall. Everything in the house was neat and clean. The furnishings were mostly old pieces, some antiques. He figured they probably came with the house when she inherited it; they looked as if they would belong to someone's maiden aunt. The kitchen was bright and cheery with a breakfast nook at one end. The back door led to a small yard with more flowers.

She guided him out of the kitchen and back into the hallway, then unfastened a bolt lock that secured a door from inside the house. "This is the room that I have available." She stepped aside and let him enter ahead of her. "Aunt Sofie used to rent the room out to summer tourists. I still do the same...occasionally." She once again felt the self-conscious flush spread across her skin. She walked across the room to the door leading out onto the front porch. "This is your entrance. You can use this way to come and go in private. This—" she indicated another door across the room "—is your private bathroom."

Trent looked around the large bedroom. Like the rest of the house, it was neat and clean. There was a large four-poster bed with a nightstand on each side, a dresser and a chest. In the corner was a large, comfortable-looking easy chair with a reading lamp. There was also a small desk and a stand with a television. A full-length mirror hung on the outside of the closet door.

"This is very nice. I'm sure I'll be very comfortable," Trent said.

His blue eyes sparkled. He had a handsome, tanned face, and his smile showed a row of perfect white teeth. His sun-streaked blond hair lay thick and full across the top of his ears and the nape of his neck, with errant strands hanging in casual disarray across his forehead.

She could not help noticing, again, how very good-looking he was. His shoulders were broad, his arms well tanned and muscular where they extended from the cut-off sleeves of his shirt.

She had never been this impulsive with anyone before, offering a complete stranger a room in her home. She knew nothing about him except that he made her insides tremble in an exciting way that she had not experienced for quite some time.

Trent deposited his suitcase in the corner of his room then followed Cassie back into the house, waiting as she secured the bolt lock on the door. He looked toward the staircase. "What's up there?"

"That's my bedroom and bathroom." She noted the sly sparkle in his eyes as she felt the flush cover her cheeks. "There's another room up there that I use as an office for keeping the books and dealing with other business connected with the restaurant and bar."

She nervously ran her fingers through her short hair. Something about the twinkle in his eyes and that damnably sexy smile of his—suddenly the house seemed very small, the space very crowded, the air almost nonexistent. Trent had neither done nor said anything improper, nothing that should have caused her alarm. She did not understand this sudden uneasiness. She tried to dismiss the feeling as just one of those things.

"Well." Her nervousness was still with her. "I need to get back to work. We have to get ready for the lunch rush and if it's anything like the breakfast crowd, we'll be very busy." She started for the front door with Trent following. "We open at five o'clock for breakfast and remain open through lunch, until two in the afternoon. The restaurant isn't open for dinner but we do serve some food, mostly sandwiches and the like, in the bar at night. Anne makes them up, wraps them and puts them in the refrigerator before she goes home.''

"Five o'clock in the morning? That's sure early. Tell me..." He allowed his voice to trail off as he again searched her eyes looking for some kind of truth. "Do you open the restaurant in the morning, work there all day, then close the bar at night? If so, that's an incredibly long day. It certainly doesn't leave you any time for a social life..." He reached out and gently brushed his fingertips across her cheek. "Or time for yourself."

Something in his eyes—she did not know what—told her he was speaking more from within himself than to her. She detected a note, just a hint, of sadness in his words. Trent Nichols was a much more complex man than she had first thought. But then she had also thought he was down on his luck without enough money to pay for his breakfast. He had, as he said he would, paid for his breakfast when he had returned with his suitcase.

His unwavering gaze made her uncomfortable; the feel of his fingertips against her skin made her tremble. She turned away and walked out on the porch. "I don't put in that long a day too often. Charlene opens up with Anne and Danny, and I come in around seven when the breakfast rush picks up. I usually take care of the books and other business after lunch. Sometimes I check in during the late afternoon and early evening and help out with happy hour, but Mike usually has things well in hand."

She directed a shy smile toward him. "You happened to catch us when Charlene was away. Her mother has been ill and she went to Tacoma to take care of her. She should be back in a few days but it has left us a little shorthanded in the meantime. It was certainly lucky for me that you showed up when you did." Her gaze dropped to the ground as a flush of embarrassment crossed her cheeks. "If you hadn't saved me from that fall I don't know what we would have done about staying open for business."

The shyness and embarrassment that now plagued her were very unusual. She was not the shy, retiring type. In fact, that was one of the things that she and Jerry, her ex-husband, had continually fought about. He wanted a quiet, stay-at-home wife who would always have dinner waiting for him no matter how late he stayed out—or with whom.

She had no proof, but she firmly believed he had been unfaithful to her on numerous occasions. She was sure he had been having an affair with the law clerk who worked in his office. She allowed a quick stab of disgust to poke at her consciousness. Lying, cheating, deceitful attorneys—none of them could be trusted. The lies were what she hated most, even more than his constant criticism of her decision to pursue her own career.

"I'm glad fate decided to intervene and direct me here." Perhaps Randall's need of a favor was, indeed, fate.

Trent's warm smile and his words, edged with an obvious sincerity, snapped her out of her moment of reflection and brought her back into the present. "Yes, well . . ." She nervously ran her fingers through her hair again. "I'd better get back to work."

Cassie had given Trent a key to his private entrance and bolted the door to his room from inside the house, thus securing the room from the rest of her living quarters. He unpacked and settled into his new surroundings after which he made several notes in a small notebook concerning the conflicting information regarding ownership of the businesses involved and Cassie's reaction to Bob Hampton and the motel.

Now that he had decided to stay and had procured a room, Trent had many details to handle. First was a discussion with the harbormaster. He paid one month in advance for docking space and an extra service charge for security and maintenance. He also provided a healthy tip for the harbormaster's discretion in keeping the transaction and identity of the yacht's owner confidential.

Trent next procured a post office box so that he could receive mail without it going to Cassie's house. He located a pay phone away from the restaurant, called his office in Beverly Hills and told them where he would be for a while, leaving instructions that he was to be contacted only through the post office box unless it was an extreme emergency.

Finally he called Randall Davies and filled him in on the situation. Based on Trent's preliminary information, Randall made the decision to turn down Bob Hampton as a client. There were just too many extenuating circumstances and questionable areas, especially with Mr. Hampton not even being available to straighten out the confusion. Randall informed Trent that he would be drafting a letter to that effect immediately and that Trent's obligation for the favor was ended.

Trent took a moment to collect his thoughts. He decided to continue with his investigation. He still felt the business, as he perceived its operation, would be a profitable investment. Besides, he found Cassie Brockton to be a delightful diversion to his wanderings, and he wanted to know more about her. Confident that he had taken care of all the loose ends, he returned to his rented room.

Trent stretched out on the bed on his back with his hands behind his head and closed his eyes. A myriad of thoughts played through his mind. He tried to make a logical picture of the puzzle pieces he had gathered but he just did not possess enough of those pieces—yet. He did not want to make Cassie suspicious by asking questions that would seem to be none of his business. He wondered when Bob Hampton would return.

About one-thirty that afternoon he wandered back to the restaurant for some lunch. Things were still busy. Cassie was bustling back and forth between the counter and the tables, trying to keep up with everything. Trent slid quietly onto the only empty counter stool and watched the nonstop activity.

She offered him a sincere, if somewhat weary smile as she hurried past carrying three plates of food. "I'll be right with you."

He returned her smile. "Take care of your other customers first. I'm in no hurry." He observed the routine of the restaurant. Cassie was trying to do it all—wait on customers, order drinks from the bar and be the cashier. It was obvious that she was shorthanded and needed some help. The restaurant would be closing in half an hour. Trent wanted to get the feel of the restaurant and bar operation, and the best way to do that would be to offer to help her with the rush.

He glanced into the bar area and saw a drink order on a tray waiting for Cassie to pick it up. He went into the room and, without Mike's noticing, grabbed the tray and carried it back through the door. He called to Cassie as she rushed past him. "Where do these go?"

Her look of surprise quickly disappeared as she offered him a grateful smile. "The table in the corner, except for the beer. It goes to the end counter stool."

He quickly dispensed the drinks, then returned the tray to the bar. Mike glared at him. "What do you think you're doing? That tray is for the restaurant drinks."

"That's what I was doing, delivering drinks," he said, then turned and left the bar. Once back in the restaurant he saw several people standing at the cash register wanting to pay their bill. He looked around. The register was one of those old-fashioned types with a No Sale key that opened the cash drawer. Cassie was in the kitchen picking up food orders.

Cassie exited the kitchen with her hands full and immediately saw Trent at the cash register, taking in money and giving out change. Her first reaction was anger. What was he doing with her money? She took a closer look and saw that he was neatly stacking money with the accompanying lunch check and dispensing the proper change but was not ringing it on the register. Had she not been so busy she would have immediately confronted this stranger who seemed to be making himself at home with her cash register. She was thankful that he had not attempted to ring up the amounts on the wrong keys. She kept a careful eye on what he was doing while continuing to take care of her customers.

The last of the rush finally died down and she was able to put the Closed sign on the restaurant door. She immediately locked the door then rang up all the lunch checks Trent had taken in while she was busy. Then she turned and glared at him.

He caught the intensity of her expression. Before she could say anything—and by the look on her face it was obvious that she fully intended to take him to task for his actions—he tried to smooth over the situation. "I know. I had no business handling the money, but you were so rushed, and you had customers waiting. I decided it made more sense to try and appease you later than to have your customers angry because they had been kept waiting when it didn't have to be that way.'' He offered her an apologetic smile.

She was not quite sure what to do. She had been fully prepared to make her displeasure known, but he had beaten her to it by apologizing before she had a chance to say anything. She did not intend to let it pass this easily, though. She would let him know exactly how she felt about his intrusion. She mustered as stern an attitude as she could, considering that his dazzling smile was making her insides melt. Her tone conveyed her displeasure. ''Look, this is my restaurant. I own it and I run it. I have enough problems with Bob Hampton butting in to my business. I don't appreciate strangers stepping in, taking over and especially handling my money without my permission.''

She continued before he could interrupt. ''I appreciate your intentions, but this is a small town. I won't lose customers just because I'm shorthanded today and they had to wait a few minutes.''

He reached out and clasped her hand in his as he looked at her for a long moment. His voice was soft, sincere. ''I was totally out of line in stepping in like that without your permission. I'm just not accustomed to small towns. Please forgive me?''

She slowly removed her hand from his electric touch. She needed to break the physical contact he had initiated between them. As much as she did not want to admit it, his touch stirred desires in her. It was those desires that had made her act impulsively in renting him the room. It was those desires that allowed her to dismiss his intrusion into her business with no more than a mild admonishment. It was those desires that caused her insides to tremble.

She retained her stern look, wanting to make sure he understood how seriously she took the matter. "Okay, you're forgiven. This time. Now, if you'll excuse me, I still have work to do."

"This time I'll ask. What do you need to do? Is there something I can help you with?" His offer was not totally without ulterior motive. He wanted to see how much money the restaurant took in for breakfast and lunch. He could see for himself that things were busy at lunch, but when he had come in earlier there were no customers at all. He wondered if it was a typical day.

"No, it's just the end-of-shift details." She began punching the total keys on the register as she continued talking. "Ringing out the register, balancing the restaurant checks against the totals, taking care of the daily bank deposit, things like that. It doesn't take very long. It's when I have to deal with the actual bookkeeping that it takes longer." She removed the cash drawer from the register, gathered up the restaurant checks and set them on the counter, then reached underneath and picked up two ledgers, placing them on top of the stack.

Trent thought back on the past half hour. He had to admit to himself that he had rather enjoyed the bustling activity and eavesdropping on the conversations between the customers—just open, friendly exchanges without the stress and pressure of needing to read between the lines to determine what was really being said, to constantly second-guess someone's real motives. It was a comfortable feeling. He reached over and picked up a newspaper someone had left on one of the bar stools.

Her voice quickly broke into his thoughts. "You're not going to throw that paper away, are you?"

A little hint of surprise covered his face. "Well, yes, I was."

She took it from him. "Never throw newspapers away. I save them for the recycle stack at the corner market." She folded the paper neatly and stuck it under the counter with several other folded newspapers.

Cassie picked up the cash drawer and the things stacked on top of it. She struggled with the awkward configuration, trying to balance everything without dropping it on the floor.

Trent moved quickly to her side. "Here, let me help you with that." He took the ledgers and restaurant checks, leaving her with the cash drawer. "Where do you want this stuff?"

His steady gaze again made her insides quiver with excitement. "Everything goes to my office." She held his gaze for a moment longer then turned and left the restaurant through the back door, with Trent following her.

In her house she climbed the stairs to the second floor, Trent's gaze glued to the fluid movements of her body as he continued to follow her. When they reached the top of the stairs he saw her office straight ahead. He glanced quickly to the right, peering through an open door into her bedroom. The room was bright and cheery. It was completely different from the rest of the house—it did not look as if it belonged to a maiden aunt. It was feminine without being frilly, the colors soft and muted. He saw a king-size bed and a dresser but did not have a chance to observe any more.

"Just put that on the table over here," Cassie said indicating the place as she entered the office.

"Is there anything I can help you with? I'm pretty handy with numbers and such." He leaned back against the table, his arms folded across his chest.

"No, thank you. This won't take me long." Her brow furrowed slightly. He may have taken it upon himself to handle the money at the register for a short period of time, but there was no reason for him to know how much money she took in for the day.

He noticed the expression. "Is there something wrong?"

A little tremor darted through her as she gave a fleeting thought to the excitement he caused in her on one hand and her wariness of him on the other. She shoved away the unwelcome intrusion. "No, it's just that it's been a hectic day. I was looking forward to a few minutes to relax with some peace and quiet."

He eyed her for a moment, then offered her his best sexy smile. "After you finish your work here, how about coming back to the bar and I'll buy you a glass of wine?"

She cocked her head to one side and studied him for a moment, wondering how much personal emphasis would be acceptable for a clearly business situation, then returned his smile. "I'd enjoy that."

He gave her a quick wink as he headed toward her office door. "It's a date."

She watched as he left the office and descended the staircase. She heard the front door close. Cassie leaned back in her chair and closed her eyes. A mental image of Trent formed on the inside of her eyelids.

Trent Nichols was a very disconcerting man. The way he made her feel inside disturbed her, but she had to admit she also liked the feeling. Her breathing increased slightly. She pictured his dazzling smile, his sparkling blue eyes...his sensuous mouth. She quickly opened her eyes and looked around, then turned her attention to the work at hand.

* * *

Trent wandered into the bar and took a seat on the end bar stool. He became immediately aware of Mike's brusque attitude and the expression on his face that clearly indicated Mike's dislike for him. He picked up another newspaper someone had left behind.

"Cassie saves those." Mike immediately jumped into the middle of what Trent was doing. "She folds them up and stores them under the counter, then when she gets a stack of them she hauls them off to the recycle place at the market." He took the paper from Trent and folded it.

"Yes, I know. She told me." He did not interfere with what Mike was doing. It was obvious Mike was establishing his authority over the happenings in the bar, not unlike an animal marking its territory.

"What'll you have?" Mike's voice was curt and his words clipped.

Trent looked around, noting that most of the afternoon customers were drinking beer, then returned his attention to Mike. "I'll have a glass of white wine."

Mike muttered under his breath as he turned to get the drink. "Humph, it figures. White wine."

Trent correctly interpreted Mike's attitude as a basic skepticism about everything, not just Trent's presence. If there was one thing that many years of a successful law practice had taught him it was to be able to size up people in a hurry.

If there was anything else he had learned, it was to keep his ears open. The local gossip turned out to be full of interesting little tidbits about the town and its people. He heard Bob Hampton's name mentioned on several occasions, and never in a favorable way. He sat quietly, sipping his wine and listening to the conversation. As with the lunch crowd in the restaurant, everyone seemed open and the life-style uncomplicated.

Then a bit of conversation floated across his consciousness and immediately grabbed his attention. Someone at a table behind him was talking about the newly arrived white yacht with the California registration that was docked in the harbor. He tried to tune in to the conversation, to catch everything that was being said, but there was too much distracting noise. He casually swiveled around on the stool to see who was talking.

"Hi." Cassie's voice interrupted his concentration.

"Hi, yourself. Shall we sit at a table?" He picked up his glass of wine and turned to Mike. "Another glass of wine, please." Trent caught Mike's look of disapproval as he rose to escort Cassie to an empty table in the corner.

As soon as they were seated she immediately commented on his proprietary manner, her voice teasing yet still conveying a hint of irritation. "You did it again."

He looked at her in surprise. "Did what?"

"Made decisions for me without consulting me first. I don't recall saying I wanted a glass of white wine."

"You look like a white wine type of person to me. Is there something you'd rather have?"

"No...it's just that I would have preferred it if you had asked me first."

He caught the hint of irritation and recalled the way she had taken him to task less than an hour ago. His response was sincere. "I'm sorry. It's a bad habit of mine. If I get out of line again, feel free to give me a swift kick in the seat of the pants." He offered his best smile and extended his hand toward her. "Forgive me?"

She returned his smile as she accepted his handshake. "Yes, once again I forgive you." She allowed a stern expression. "But this is the last time."

He took a sip of his wine as Mike set a glass in front of Cassie, shot Trent a sideways glare and returned to the bar. As soon as Mike was out of earshot Trent engaged Cassie in conversation, hoping to elicit some information about her business operation. "That was a pretty good rush of business at lunch and it looks like quite a few customers in here right now. Are things always this busy?"

"Things get busier as we get into the summer season. Being right next to the ferryboat dock has its blessings and its curses. Once people have their cars in line, they end up in here while waiting for time to load. That gives us a lot of extra business but also some pretty hectic moments. I always need additional help during the summer tourist season." She allowed a slight grin to turn the corners of her mouth. "In fact, I was going to offer you a job until you insisted on paying for your breakfast when you came back with your suitcase." She felt a flush come to her cheeks as she lowered her gaze. "I thought you were out of money and looking for work. After you told me you weren't staying at the motel, I assumed you had gone there looking for a job."

Once again she had said something that caught him totally by surprise. The idea that she had planned to offer him a job for no more reason than she had assumed he was out of work and down on his luck was a totally unexpected turn of events. Cassie Brockton was certainly a very special lady. He reached out and lightly touched her cheek, his fingertips lingering for a moment as he captured her look. His voice was soft, conveying the sincerity of his words. "That's very gracious of you. It's not often that one finds someone who's willing to go out of their way for a stranger.''

She quickly lowered her gaze as she felt the flush again cover her cheeks. "Please, you're embarrassing me."

She appeared to have let down her guard a little. She had brought up the subject of the motel; it gave him his opening to ask about it. "You seem to be having problems with the motel owner. You mentioned something earlier about him continually butting in to your business."

A quick look of anger again flashed across her face, and her tone of voice indicated her displeasure. "Bob Hampton!"

There it was again, her antagonism toward Bob Hampton. He took a chance on a casual question, hoping it would not further anger her. "Why would you have problems with this guy? If you own this business what makes him think he has anything to say about your operation?"

She eyed him carefully for a minute. Bob had been up to something lately and she did not know what. She felt a wariness about this stranger who had so subtly moved into her life. Did he have some connection with the motel and with Bob Hampton? She carefully weighed her words, then spoke. "You seem to have quite a bit of interest in the motel. Do you know Bob Hampton?" She paused a moment before continuing. "Are you a business associate of his?"

Trent's answer was straightforward, regardless of what was going on inside his head. "I've never met him. I was just curious, that's all."

She did not know whether to believe his answer or not. Well, if he did know Bob then he already knew what she was about to tell him, so there would not be any harm done. "I own this building and the business operating inside it, and I own the house I live in but Bob Hampton owns the land underneath it. My aunt Sofie signed a ninety-nine-year lease on this half of the land with Bob's mother twenty-five years ago."

So that was it. Bob owned all the land and the motel, but there was a long-term lease on the half of the land containing the restaurant and Cassie's house. No wonder he had been vague about the circumstances with Randall. Bob Hampton was trying to pull something. He was probably trying to sell off everything without her knowing about it. Trent needed to somehow get his hands on a copy of the lease. He wanted to know just how things stood legally, what provisions there might have been to cover this situation.

Three

"That makes sense. I'm glad I turned him down."

"It could really be a nice little operation if handled properly. I'm going to stick around for a while and scope it out. I've rented a room from Cassie Brockton, the owner of the restaurant. That puts me in a pretty good position to observe what's going on. I might want to go through you to make this Bob Hampton some kind of an offer. I'll keep in touch." Trent placed the phone receiver in its cradle.

His conversation with Randall Davies had been very brief and to the point. He left the pay phone he had found a block away from Cassie's house and returned to his rented room, removed the notebook from the desk drawer and made several notations, then replaced it. He reflected over the two hours he and Cassie had spent together that afternoon.

She was articulate, witty, charming and comfortable to be around without being full of pretenses. She also had a feisty independence that he admired, even if they had crossed swords a couple of times during their brief acquaintance. He was still surprised at the way she had berated him for taking the initiative and helping out at lunch. He had assumed she would be grateful for the assistance rather than angry.

He flipped on the television and watched the evening news but could not get interested in any of the evening programs. He wondered where Cassie was and what she was doing. A restlessness gripped him. He finally snapped off the television and left his room.

Trent wandered over to the motel and walked completely around it, looking in windows wherever possible and generally giving it a close inspection. It would need a lot of work, but he could clearly visualize the results. The more he contemplated the possibilities, the more he warmed to the idea. He left the motel and walked along the sidewalk in front of the restaurant, headed toward the waterfront.

Cassie stood just outside the bar entrance, watching him. She was just leaving after having checked on Mike to see if he needed any help. How curious it was, the way Trent had seemed to be inspecting the motel property in great detail. His actions were very suspicious. Something was going on. He had said he did not know Bob Hampton, but she was beginning to wonder if that was true.

"Trent." She called out to him, noting the startled expression on his face when he saw her.

"Cassie..." He wondered how long she had been standing there, whether or not she had been watching him. "I didn't see you there." He walked up the path toward the bar. Indicating the front door, he asked, "Are you coming or going?"

"I was just leaving. I always check in with Mike about this time to see if he needs help." She hesitated for a moment, then continued. "Did I see you coming from the motel? It's still closed, isn't it?"

"I was just looking it over. Curiosity following our conversation. It's very close to summer season. Shouldn't it be open for business?"

"It used to be open year-round. I'm not sure what Bob Hampton's up to or where he's gone." She eyed him warily. "You seem a lot more interested than just idle curiosity."

He offered her another one of his dazzling smiles. "I was about to take a walk along the waterfront, look around a bit. Could I persuade you to join me?" He had abruptly changed the subject, she noted, as if he didn't want to continue with her train of thought or where it might lead.

"No... I have some work to do in my office. Maybe some other time."

"Okay. I'll see you later." He stuck his hands into his pockets and casually strolled across the street and down the block.

Cassie returned to her office and tried to concentrate on the stack of papers on her desk. Her mind kept wandering back to Trent and their conversations. He was definitely being very secretive about something, and whatever it was, it was sending signals of caution racing through her body.

It was late when Trent returned to Cassie's house, letting himself into his room through his private entrance. He had noticed the lights shining through the curtains of the second-floor windows. She was still up. It had been a long day and he was tired.

He had just pulled off his shirt when there was a knock at his door. He heard the click as she released the bolt lock on her side so he could open the door.

Cassie's jeans and crisp blouse were gone and in their place was a long velour robe in a rich peacock blue with white lace at the neck and the cuffs of the long sleeves. She was barefoot, her toenails painted a pale coral shade that matched the color dotted on her soft lips. She was enticingly sexy, despite the fact that the robe was in no way revealing.

Her hair was still slightly damp and she smelled of a light rose scent, a sweet but clean fragrance. She had obviously just gotten out of the bathtub and was ready for bed. He felt a slight rush as he looked into her hazel eyes. There was something so real, so honest about her. He had an overwhelming desire to sweep her into his arms and kiss her very tempting mouth. He managed to keep his errant desires in check.

Trent stood before her wearing only his jeans. His chest was as tanned as his face and arms. His body was taut and athletic without being overly muscular. It took all her willpower to keep from reaching out and touching the sandy-colored hair that curled across his hard chest in perfect symmetry, a thin trail angling downward until it became lost from sight in his jeans.

The way his clear blue eyes looked her over then settled their gaze on her eyes made her insides jump—again. It was very unsettling, this feeling that came over her every time they were together. "I, uh, knocked on your door an hour ago. I guess you were out."

"I just got back from my walk." His voice softened as he reflected on his wanderings along the waterfront.

"Just trying to sort out some things, determine some priorities."

She nervously ran her fingers through her short hair. "I, uh, just wanted to see if you needed anything before I turned in for the night. Do you have enough towels?" The butterflies flitted around inside her stomach as she looked into his steady gaze. She felt drawn to him, like a moth to a flame. Their proximity caused shivers of excitement to dart through her as her breathing increased slightly.

The air was thick with their combined desires, an unmistakable electricity that neither could deny even if they had wanted to.

She wanted to touch him, to feel his lips on hers, to taste his kiss. The situation was, of course, totally preposterous. He was a complete stranger. She knew nothing about him—not even where he came from. She had already exhibited truly outlandish behavior by renting him a room. But there was something about him that made her throw caution to the wind, something that made her feel adventurous and free spirited, something that made her want to explore all the feelings he stirred in her.

He was experiencing very similar sensations, and they were creating an awkward situation for him. He was living under Cassie's roof but was evaluating the possibility of taking over the restaurant and motel operation as a personal investment. It was beginning to seem like a bad idea, poor judgment on his part to have established a personal relationship with one of the involved parties.

He cautiously reached his hand toward her face, lightly touched the silky smoothness of her cheek with his fingertips then quickly withdrew his hand. The words popped into his head, as bold and loud as if he had actually spoken them for all to hear. "Oh, what a tangled web we weave..."

He wanted to stop the deception right now, tell her the truth before it grew to such proportions that it became thoroughly entrenched, driving an invisible wedge between them. He wanted to, but he could not.

He wanted to know everything about her, know her intellectually, emotionally... and intimately. He knew if he was to reveal who he was, what he did for a living and why he was there that he would be put into a position where he would be forced to leave—especially in light of her very low opinion of attorneys.

Cassie shivered with anticipation. Her curiosity and her desires could no longer be held in. She stood on her toes and reached her face up to his, placing a kiss on his lips. She felt a moment's hesitation on his part, a fleeting hint of uncertainty, then he returned her kiss. His mouth was every bit as sensual as she had imagined, his kiss every bit as exciting. She did not put her arms around him; only their lips came in physical contact. She had not been able to resist the overwhelming temptation a moment longer.

Her sudden aggression startled him, made him hesitate for just a moment before he returned the softness of her kiss. Following her lead, he did not enfold her in his embrace or touch her in any way other than the kiss. He wanted to twine his fingers in her hair, to dart his tongue into the sweetness of her mouth and feel the soft texture he knew must be hidden there. He wanted to but he did not. Again he kept his own desires in check.

Cassie pulled back from his face and looked into his eyes, the clear, sky blue color having darkened into an intense smoldering blue. The room seemed to crackle with electrical energy. Her words were tinged with just a hint of huskiness and an embarrassed hesitation. "I, uh . . ." She allowed her gaze to drop to the floor for a moment before returning to the intensity of his blue eyes. "I've been wondering what kissing you would be like ever since I fell off the ladder and into your arms. I don't need to speculate about it anymore. Now the curiosity is satisfied and the temptation out of the way."

Trent lay in bed staring up at the ceiling. He had been unable to fall asleep, to even force his eyes closed. He had never had that happen to him in just that way—it was all so straightforward and honest, no silly games or pretenses. Each had felt the pull of the other and both were curious about exploring that magnetism. She had taken the initiative and been the aggressor. As she had said, now the curiosity was put to rest and things could move along, without the nagging question always being at the back of their minds.

That was what she had said, all right, the only problem being that it put nothing to rest as far as Trent was concerned. From the moment her lips brushed lightly against his, before coming to rest on his mouth, he knew he wanted much more of her. Her taste was every bit as sweet as he had known it would be, every bit as exciting. He wondered if she was having as much trouble falling asleep as he was. A little tremor darted through his body as he wondered what he had gotten himself into and if he would ever be able to straighten out the truth.

He shoved the disturbing thoughts from his mind and turned his attention to the business at hand. He tried to make an estimate of the dollar amount taken in at the restaurant and at the bar. He wondered if it had been a typical business day. He needed to get a look at her books.

* * *

Cassie was every bit as awake as Trent. The feel of his lips against hers remained emblazoned on her mind. The initial curiosity had, indeed, been satisfied but the temptation was now stronger than ever. It had been an awkward moment when Trent had moved to embrace her. She had stepped back, avoiding his arms, and had seen the surprise and confusion on his face. Neither of them had said anything as they looked into each other's eyes for a long moment. It was Cassie who had turned away first.

Her voice had been soft and filled with the emotion of the moment as she had tried to put things back on a more impersonal level. "Good night, Trent. I'll see you in the morning."

"Good night, Cassie."

One thought had kept running through her mind as she had climbed the stairs to her bedroom. Who was Trent Nichols and why was he on her island?

"Mike tells me you've rented out your spare room to some stranger who wandered in yesterday morning. That was a pretty impulsive decision, wasn't it?" There was a note of caution in Jake's voice as he sipped his coffee.

"Mike worries too much." She tried to project a casual manner, treating the situation in a light-spirited vein. "Trent is very nice, and besides, for reasons unknown, Bob seems to have the motel closed. I can use the extra money. It's no different than when Aunt Sofie would rent the room out to strangers. The inside door to the room locks from inside my house so that he only has access to his room from the porch, without being able to go into the rest of the house." She quickly remembered that the door had not been bolted last night. When she had gone back to her room she had not bothered locking it.

"Where is he? I'd like to meet this stranger who has apparently turned your normally sensible head."

Cassie laughed as she poured more coffee into Jake's mug then glanced at the clock on the wall. "Stop letting Mike influence you before you've even met Trent. He'll probably be in for breakfast. You can inspect him then."

"I'm not trying to pry into your business but, well, it's just that Mike doesn't seem to care for the guy very much—thinks he's hiding something. I think you should be cautious, that's all. I don't trust Bob Hampton. This guy could be someone Bob sent here to undermine your operation. You know your lease is the only thing that's kept him from selling everything. He hasn't figured out how to get around it . . . yet."

Their conversation was interrupted by Trent's voice as he entered the restaurant. "Good morning, Cassie."

"Good morning," she said, smiling. Their gazes locked for a brief moment before she turned her head toward Jake. "Trent, this is Jake Dorsey. Jake, this is Trent Nichols. He's rented my spare room for the duration of his visit on the island." The two men shook hands.

"Nice to meet you, Jake." Trent seated himself on the next stool and took a sip of the coffee Cassie had just poured for him.

Jake carefully engaged Trent in casual conversation. A little frown crossed Jake's brow. Something about the situation bothered him, but he could not quite put his finger on exactly what it was. Trent artfully managed to sidestep every one of Jake's direct questions about what he did for a living, where he came from and why he had picked this particular location to visit, without being even the slightest bit offensive with his answers. There was no doubt in Jake's mind that Trent was a very smooth character, but was it because he was hiding something, or was he merely being polite about letting Jake know that the personal information was none of his business?

The restaurant business slowed down to the midmorning crawl. Trent and Jake had been carrying on a conversation through the morning. Cassie kept glancing at the clock. Mike was late, which was very unlike him. It was almost eleven o'clock and Jake and Trent were the only customers in the restaurant, so Cassie went into the bar to begin setting it up for lunch.

About ten minutes later Mike came in the door. All it took was one quick glance to determine that he had no business being at work. His eyes were red and watery, his skin dry and pale. He started to tell Cassie he was sorry he was late, but his raspy voice could not get all the words out.

Cassie immediately rushed to his side and put her hand on his forehead. "You're running a temperature. What are you doing here? You should be home in bed. Now turn around and get out of here."

Mike carefully eyed Trent sitting at the counter, obviously listening to their conversation. "With Charlene gone, it would leave you impossibly shorthanded. I can get through the day okay."

"No way. We just won't open the bar until the restaurant closes at two o'clock. That way I'll only have to do drinks for the restaurant customers. If you refuse to consider your own health, then think about my customers." She gave him a teasing grin. "How can they come in here and spend their money if you give all of them the flu and they have to stay home sick? Now—" she physically turned him toward the door "—go home."

Mike again tossed a very suspicious look Trent's way then turned toward her. "Are you sure you can manage?"

"I'm positive. Now get out of here. If you need anything, give me a call." She watched as Mike reluctantly made his way back out the door and walked down the street to his small house a couple of blocks away.

Cassie turned toward Jake with a questioning look. "What's on your schedule for today? Do you think you could help me in the bar until I close the restaurant?"

She saw the disappointment cross his face. "I'm sorry, Cassie. I've got a fishing charter to take out in half an hour. Otherwise, you know I'd do it."

Trent, who had been carefully following the conversation, spoke up. "I'd be happy to help you. I don't have anything special planned for the day."

She eyed him carefully. "Do you know how to tend bar?"

"As long as no one orders one of those obscure drinks with half a dozen ingredients that's made in the blender and is topped off by a basket of fruit and an umbrella."

She laughed an open, easy laugh. "Not around here. An occasional martini, but nothing more difficult than that. It's mostly beer, wine and well drinks." She looked up into his eyes, the smile fading from her face. "Are you sure you don't mind? I don't expect you to do it for free. I will, of course, pay you for a bar shift." Their gazes locked again as a sensual electricity danced between them.

"That won't be necessary. I'm happy to be able to help out..." he regained his composure and flashed her his dazzling smile "...without you getting mad at me." He saw the color tinge her cheeks as she lowered her eyelids.

Jake rose from the counter seat, took the last swallow of his coffee and headed for the door. He shot a questioning look in Trent's direction, then addressed his comments to Cassie. "I'll check in with you later."

"Okay, Jake."

She then turned her attention to Trent. "Come on, I'll show you where everything is and how it functions."

Before they could get to the bar, the restaurant door opened and a man entered. She had never seen him before. He walked to the cash register and stood there, not taking a seat at the counter. Cassie hurried behind the counter. She quickly looked him over. He wore a suit, but it was ill fitting and wrinkled, the jacket sleeves and trouser cuffs were frayed and his shoes needed to be shined.

He looked her up and down then spoke, his voice carrying just a hint of superiority. "Is the boss man in?"

"May I help you?" Her muscles tensed slightly at his tone of voice, and her jaw tightened almost imperceptibly.

"No, girlie. I need to speak to the man in charge."

Trent's senses were on alert as he listened to the exchange and read the body language of Cassie and the man. His initial instinct was to intervene, to take charge of the situation and stop this man from harassing her, but he held his tongue. This was Cassie's business; she was in charge. It was up to her to handle the situation. She had already made it abundantly clear to him that she did not appreciate his interference in things that were none of his business. So he just stood there and listened.

Cassie stared at the man, looking him right in the eye. "I'm the *person* in charge. What is it you want?"

"No, girlie." His voice clearly showed his irritation at her apparent inability to understand what he wanted. "I want to talk to the man who owns this place."

Cassie took a calming breath to steady her mounting anger. "My name is not 'girlie' and *I* happen to own this establishment. Now, what is it you want?"

He immediately attempted to correct his mistake. He smiled, removed a business card from his jacket pocket and handed it to Cassie. "Name's Hemple. Couldn't help noticing that your building here needs some repair work. Roof looks like it has some bad spots, sides need painting, rain gutters need repairing—"

"Mr. Hemple." Trent's voice broke into the conversation. "Do you have a contractor's license? We couldn't possibly consider availing ourselves of your services without having your license number and checking it out with the state agency who issued it. We'd also like a list of references, people you've provided contracting services for in the last several months." Without being consciously aware of it Trent had slipped into his best legal interrogation mode. His questions were precise, his words clipped. His manner was intended to intimidate.

Cassie looked at Trent, a combination of mounting anger and curiosity covering her features. She allowed a slight frown. For a moment he had almost sounded like the prosecutor at a trial, cross-examining a witness.

"Look here, fella." Hemple turned his attention to Trent, not quite knowing what to make of the situation. "The girlie and I are having a business conversation."

Trent leveled a steady look at Mr. Hemple, his intense blue eyes boring into the man's being. He gestured toward Cassie. "This is a lady, not—"

Cassie's voice took control of the situation before the exchange of words got out of hand. "The 'girlie' and you have concluded this conversation. Your services are not required. Goodbye." She glared at the man. He looked back at her, glanced at Trent then turned and left the restaurant.

She turned her attention to Trent, who immediately allowed his gaze to drop to the floor as he shifted his weight from one foot to the other. He never should have spoken up the way he did, but it had irritated him the way the guy had talked to Cassie, treating her as if she was some bimbo. He was obviously a con artist who made his living by talking small business owners into signing for repairs, then ripping them off.

"That was quite a little speech. Once again, *Mr. Nichols,* you seem to have appointed yourself the person in charge of my business dealings." Cassie's voice clearly conveyed her resentment at this most recent intrusion. But there was more. . . . "You sounded like you knew exactly what you were talking about, like you had participated in similar conversations at other times." She allowed a frown to furrow her brow and her jaw to tighten. "You sounded just like—" she paused, then spit out the word as if it were poison "—an attorney."

He inwardly flinched at her tone of voice. Her contempt and disgust for anything associated with an attorney was blatantly obvious. He knew he had been wrong to interfere, knew that he would probably incur her wrath, but he felt an overwhelming need to protect her. From the moment she had fallen into his arms he had felt a sense of responsibility for her well-being.

He looked up and smiled, trying to recover from his impulsive error. He did not like the angry sparks that seemed to flash from her eyes. "Comes from watching too much television, especially police and lawyer shows. I just gave him my best Sergeant Joe Friday," he said,

adopting a thoughtful expression. "Or maybe it was
Perry Mason." He extended the pleading look of a little
boy who had been caught with his hand in the cookie jar
and knew he was going to be punished. "I'm sorry. It was
just that he was so obviously a con man trying to rip you
off."

Her tone of voice was still angry. "And you thought I
wasn't smart enough to figure that out?"

Four

Trent reached out and touched her cheek. "Not at all. I find you very intelligent." He searched the depths of her hazel eyes as he cupped her face in his hands and lowered his head to hers. "And very desirable."

Before she could stop him, Cassie felt his mouth on hers, felt the heat of his kiss. All her anger disappeared in a puff of smoke, a puff of smoke that bordered on being an incendiary ball of fire. The kiss did not last that long, only a few seconds, but it scorched right through to her soul. She was incapable of putting up even the slightest resistance.

His voice was soft. "Once again I'm sorry for interfering with your business." His fingers lightly traced the outline of her lips. "I seem to always be apologizing to you."

She tried to regain control, not only of her emotions but also control of the situation. She stepped away from his mesmerizing presence, nervously ran her fingers through her hair and took a calming breath. "It's...it's because you keep doing things that require an apology."

He allowed a teasing grin to turn the corners of his mouth. "I guess it's just my naturally pushy manner."

"Well, maybe that works wherever you come from, but it doesn't work around here." She turned and headed toward the bar. "There's work to do and it's almost lunchtime." He followed her. The heated moment had passed.

Cassie made no mention of his kiss, gave no indication of how it had affected her. She went through the cash register procedures with him, showed him where things were stored and filled him in on the regular customers he would probably encounter. After that she returned to the restaurant to prepare for the lunch crowd.

"It's been quite a morning so far." Anne spoke up from the door to the kitchen.

Cassie glanced curiously toward the bar, then returned her attention to Anne. "It certainly hasn't been dull."

"Do you want me to call my niece to help with the lunch rush? She could probably be here in fifteen minutes."

"I think we'll probably be able to make it okay. Today hasn't been the rush we had yesterday, so far. I'm sure we'll be fine."

Fortunately Cassie's words were true. Lunch was not the hassled rush of the day before. Cassie bustled from table to counter but was able to keep up with the customers. In addition to the drink orders coming from the restaurant, Trent had several bar customers but was able to handle it all without too many problems.

Finally two o'clock arrived and Cassie put out the Closed sign and locked the restaurant entrance, then went into the bar. "How's it going?"

Trent offered a weary smile. "It's been a little hectic, but everything's okay. Now that I've gotten the hang of the routine, this evening should go much easier for me."

Her surprise was evident. "What do you mean, this evening?"

"You can't work from five o'clock this morning until late tonight and then again at five o'clock tomorrow morning. You'll end up collapsing from exhaustion."

"Look—"

His expression was stern as he cut off her words. "No, you look. I'm right and you know it. Now, there's no reason why I can't finish out the day here. You go and take care of your restaurant business and I'll take care of the bar business." He stood his ground, not backing down from her angry glare.

Cassie started to say something, started to vent her anger over his totally unacceptable behavior, but she stopped herself. She weighed his words. In spite of his pushiness she did have to admit to herself that what he said made sense. She let out a sigh as her anger subsided. "I'm going to tend to the restaurant close-out then I have some personal business to handle. We'll discuss who's working tonight later."

Cassie took the cash drawer from the restaurant and went to her office. She quickly dispensed with her bookkeeping chores, prepared her bank deposit, checked her list of errands, then leaned back in the chair and closed her eyes. Her thoughts were on Trent Nichols and the excitement he stirred in her whenever he was near. No matter how angry he made her, it seemed that all he needed to do was touch her cheek and her anger dissolved. She remembered the kiss they had shared earlier, the heat of his barely concealed passion.

She had thought her life was finally running in a smooth and orderly fashion. She liked living on the island, did not miss the big-city hassle of Chicago or the stress and pressure of her banking career. Things were so straightforward and honest; everyone and everything was exactly who and what they appeared to be. Then this stranger shows up from out of nowhere and...

Cassie did not return to the bar until almost six o'clock that evening. Things were much busier than she thought they would be. Trent was swamped as he tried to mix drinks and wait on tables all at the same time. She immediately took over the tables and caught him up on washing the dirty glasses. She made a mental note to have a dishwasher installed in the bar. Mike had mentioned it when she had had the dishwasher installed in the kitchen, but she had not realized the necessity until she saw the backlog of dirty glasses. Since Trent was by himself and unaccustomed to working in a bar, he did not have time to wash them while mixing drinks and waiting on tables. Business stayed brisk all evening.

Cassie continued to help Trent until they finally closed at eleven-thirty. After locking the bar door behind the last customer she plopped down on a stool and breathed a sigh of relief. "Wow! That was quite a rush. There's probably some sort of corollary between being short-handed and having a sudden increase in business."

"I'll buy you a drink." He reached for a wineglass, then stopped and turned to her. "What would you like?"

She looked at him for a minute then managed a weary smile. "Well, at least you asked this time. However, I'm so tired that a drink would probably put me to sleep before I can get to bed.'' Their eyes locked together, and she became aware of her own increased pulse rate.

Trent poured her a glass of wine in spite of her less than positive response and set it in front of her then poured one for himself. He took a sip as he watched her stifle a yawn. His voice was soft, almost a caress. ''You must be beyond exhaustion.''

He reached out and lightly touched her cheek, then dropped his hand to the bar, resting it next to hers. ''Would you like me to help you out in the restaurant in the morning? I could open if you'd like. It would give you a chance to get an extra couple of hours of sleep.''

''I can't do that. It's my responsibility to open the restaurant.'' She was more than aware of his touch as he slowly laced their fingers together. With her other hand she lifted her glass to her lips and sipped the wine.

Trent, too, took a sip of his wine. Their eyes met across the rim of the glasses. He watched as she lowered the glass from her mouth. He set his glass on the bar and leaned his face toward hers until their lips brushed. He brought his mouth fully against hers.

Cassie was not sure what to do, how to respond. He excited her senses as no one ever had before and caused very disconcerting emotions to well up inside her being. She did not want Trent to get the wrong idea about her, to think she was some sort of love-starved creature who would easily fall prey to his charms. Or, worse yet, that she was easily swayed by every stranger who crossed her path.

She allowed herself to briefly return his kiss before pulling her face away. Her words were barely above a whisper. ''It's late and I need to be up very early.''

''You're right.'' He again leaned his face into hers and captured her mouth with a kiss that, while soft, spoke emotional volumes about the sensuality of the man whose lips were pressed against hers.

She felt a shortness of breath and palpitations of her heart as the intensity of the kiss deepened. Now she wanted—no, make that needed—to explore the sensations he created in her. In the dimness of the bar, Cassie seated on a bar stool leaning across the bar and Trent standing behind the bar leaning forward, she returned the barely hidden passion of his kiss. In the distance a ship's horn could be heard. All else was silent except for the sound of their breathing.

Trent felt the heat of her energy as she returned his kiss. Her taste was intoxicating, almost addictive, as he cautiously darted his tongue into the tenderness of her mouth. She did not pull away from him. With their fingers still entwined he took his free hand and caressed the softness of her cheek.

He felt torn between two dynamics—his rapidly building desire for her and his discomfort about his deception and the plans that had been formulating in the back of his mind. He knew who he was and he knew who she was—she, however, did not have a clue as to who he was, where he came from or what he really wanted. She was accepting him on his word and trusting him on blind faith and instinct.

She drew her mouth away from his as she ended the kiss, leaving just the barest touch of contact lingering between their lips. It was late and this could only lead to something that should not be happening. Her voice was a mere whisper. "This . . . this isn't a good idea." She quickly recovered her composure, and her voice took on more of a tone of authority. "It's very late and I'm tired."

Trent, not wanting the kiss to end, allowed his lips to brush against hers for just a second longer. Slowly he released her hand from his grasp and stood up straight. His voice clearly conveyed the unsettling effect the kiss had had on him. "Yes . . . it's very late."

Cassie efficiently went about the business of ringing out the register and removing the cash drawer, setting it on the bar top. Trent turned out the lights, except for the night-light behind the bar, then he double-checked the lock on the front door. Cassie took the cash drawer and Trent picked up the half-full wineglasses. They exited through the back door, Cassie making sure it was securely locked.

They walked up the path to the house and he waited as she unlocked the front door. "It's a nice night out. Why don't we sit on the porch swing while we finish our wine?"

She regarded him and his request cautiously. "I don't know, it's awfully late."

He gave her a smile of encouragement. "Just until we finish our glass of wine?" He took the cash drawer from her and set it on the table inside the front door.

She moved toward the swing. "Okay, for a few minutes."

They sat next to each other, the swing gently swaying back and forth. "I can see why you like living here. It's very comfortable, very real. . . ." His voice trailed off as he stopped talking, afraid that he might already have said too much.

She immediately picked up on his words and his hesitation. "Very real—that's an odd thing to say." She turned her face toward him, his features outlined in the light of the full moon. "Where do you come from, Trent? Where have you lived that was not real?"

"I was referring to the people as much as the place. Real people without pretenses. Even Mike—he doesn't like me and he makes no effort to hide the fact. I much prefer that to someone who smiles at my face while twisting the knife in my back."

She swallowed the last sip of her wine and set the glass on the window ledge next to the swing. Again she faced him, studying his handsome features in the silvery moonlight. "Who are you, Trent Nichols?" Her gaze held his, her eyes searching for his hidden truth.

"I'm ... I don't know. I used to know but I don't anymore. Somewhere along the way I seem to have lost myself."

The statement was confusing. She was not sure exactly what he meant or what he was talking about. She did know one thing, though. It meant a lot more than the surface words would indicate. Somehow the words had come from deep inside him. Had he experienced such turmoil in his life that he had decided to simply drop out? Was that why he had wandered to the island, seeking some type of sanctuary? She closed her eyes and leaned her head back.

Trent was lost in his own thoughts for several minutes. He gradually became aware that her head was resting on his shoulder. Cassie was asleep, her breathing slow and even. Moving slowly and carefully so he would not wake her, he gently lifted her in his arms and carried her inside the house, up the stairs and to her bedroom. He placed her on the bed, removed her shoes and covered her with a blanket.

He hurried downstairs, locked the front door and brought the cash drawer up to her office. He was not sure exactly what it was she did with the cash register tape, the bar checks and the cash drawer, so he left them on the table.

He paused at her bedroom door on the way to his room, then again entered her bedroom. "Good night, Cassie." The words were said as a mere whisper. His gaze lingered on her face for a moment longer, then he reached next to her bed and shut off her alarm clock. He knew he was going to be in trouble with her again, but she needed the sleep.

"Trent!" Anne was obviously surprised by his appearance at four-forty-five in the morning as she unlocked the back door of the restaurant. She glanced back toward the house. "Is Cassie all right?"

"She opened up yesterday morning at five o'clock and closed up last night at almost midnight. She's getting some much-needed sleep." Trent himself had gotten very little sleep, maybe three hours in total. Even though he had been very tired when he climbed into bed, he had not been able to force himself to sleep. The kiss they had shared in the bar continued to play across his senses, and the feel of her snuggled in his arms as he carried her upstairs was still very real, as real as the memory of her cradled in his arms after her fall from the ladder.

Anne glanced at his empty hands. "You forgot the cash drawer. You'd better hurry back and get it. We open for business in fifteen minutes."

The cash drawer—he had not given it a thought. He knew where the drawer from the bar register was—he had put it on the table in Cassie's office—but the cash drawer from the restaurant was a different story. He quickly entered the house through his bedroom and went upstairs to the office, being very quiet so that he would not disturb her sleep. After five minutes of opening desk drawers and filing-cabinet drawers he finally found it on a shelf in the closet. He hurried back to the restaurant.

Trent was not sure exactly what the opening-up procedures for the restaurant were so he busied himself doing what he thought were the most logical things—making coffee, setting out cream pitchers and filling water glasses with ice. Jake was outside waiting as Trent unlocked the front door at five o'clock. Trent gave him a friendly smile. "Good morning, Jake. How are you today?"

"Good morning." Jake's manner was reserved, his look one of caution. "Where's Cassie?"

"She's exhausted. Hopefully she's getting some much-needed sleep."

"I see...." Jake's voice trailed off as he stared out the window at the young man swaggering up the walkway toward the restaurant. "Damn! Here comes nothing but trouble."

Trent looked out the window, following Jake's gaze. "That guy walking this way? Who is he?"

"That's Bob Hampton." Jake's immediate thought was to see if there were any signs of recognition between the two men, despite Trent's words. "He owns the land under this restaurant. The kid's a real bad apple. He'll try to bully you into what he wants. Cassie stands up to him pretty good."

Trent's brow was furrowed in thought. So, the elusive Bob Hampton had finally made an appearance.

The young man walked through the door and directly to the cash register as he looked around. "Where's Cassie?"

Trent made an immediate judgment concerning the brash young man standing before him. He was in his early twenties and wore the smug expression of someone who thought he knew it all. Trent had seen it many times before, on the faces of the spoiled adult children of many of his wealthy Beverly Hills clients. It was an attitude, a demeanor that thoroughly rankled him.

"She'll be in later. Is there something I can do for you?"

Bob Hampton looked Trent over then dismissed him as someone who was merely hired help, not noticing the quick tightening of his jaw and the narrowing of his eyes. "My business is with Cassie. Tell her to call me as soon as she gets here."

Trent maintained an expressionless mask, feigning ignorance of the situation. "Very well—can I have your name? Do you have a business card I can pass on to her?" He saw Bob's jaw tighten at the realization that this stranger did not know who he was.

His words were angry, his irritation at having to identify himself clearly evident. "Just tell her Bob Hampton wants to talk to her."

Trent grabbed a piece of paper and a pencil and made an elaborate show of jotting down the name, then crumpled the sheet of paper and threw it away as he watched Bob's stormy departure. Trent's eyes were a hard icy blue and his jaw was tightly clenched.

If there had been any lingering doubts or concerns about the plans he had been formulating, they were now resolved. Not only had this loudmouth been giving Cassie a bad time, he had now made an enemy of Trent. There was no doubt in Trent's mind that, one way or the other, he would see to it that Bob Hampton would no longer be a problem in Cassie's life. The sounds of barely suppressed chuckles reached his ears, causing him to turn toward Jake.

Jake was, indeed, trying his best to suppress his laughter. He had been carefully following the entire exchange between Bob and Trent and had come to the conclusion that the two men did not know each other. The cold, hard look in Trent's eyes as he watched Bob leave the restaurant had said it all. But it also said something else—it said that Trent was someone who was not accustomed to being talked to in that manner or in being dismissed as someone unimportant. There was definitely more to Trent Nichols than was apparent on the surface.

He looked at Trent with new admiration. "That was a good one. There's nothing that riles that little punk more than to have someone not know who he is." Jake laughed out loud as he reached forward and extended his hand to Trent. The two men shook hands, the beginnings of a new friendship forming between them in spite of Jake's concerns.

"I've been trying to get Cassie to take that lease agreement to a lawyer and have it looked over and thoroughly analyzed, but she refuses." Jake leaned forward to Trent and lowered his voice. "She used to be married to a lawyer and says she'd rather trust the devil than trust another lawyer." He did not notice the quick look of anxiety that darted across Trent's face.

The myriad of thoughts that immediately consumed Trent were interrupted by the early-morning regulars arriving for breakfast. He took Jake's order, poured him some coffee, then waited on the new arrivals as they seated themselves at the counter.

"How dare you do that to me!" It was almost nine-thirty when Cassie entered the restaurant, her words emphatic and very angry.

He wheeled around and met her gaze, her hazel eyes flashing fire. She quickly closed the distance between them, lowering her voice so the customers could not hear. "How dare you take over my business like this. At first I thought I had turned off the alarm then forgotten about it and fallen back asleep, but then I decided you had obviously turned it off when you apparently carried me upstairs."

He glared back at her. "You needed the sleep and you know it. If you weren't so pigheaded you'd admit it."

They locked horns, neither giving an inch as they continued their heated exchange of words. "I'm pigheaded? Look who's talking! How many times have I told you to stop making my business decisions?"

"If you'd use a little more common sense I wouldn't have to step in to protect you from yourself."

"And just who appointed you my protector?"

His manner softened as he reached out and gently caressed her cheek with his fingertips. He had known she was going to be angry with him. He had been prepared for her reaction. "I appointed myself to that position the moment you fell off that ladder and into my arms."

He saw a flush cover her cheeks and embarrassment come into her eyes, replacing the anger. "Actually, it's been a fairly quiet morning. Business has been steady, just enough to keep busy, but not hectic. There was one thing." His brow wrinkled in thought. "Bob Hampton said he wanted to see you."

Cassie's anger immediately flared again at the mention of the name. "That insufferable little jerk. I wonder what he wants now."

Jake sat on the end bar stool sipping his beer. "Did you and Trent get your little difference straightened out?"

Cassie frowned as she wiped off the bar. "Not exactly. I think we sort of called it a draw and let it drop... for the moment." She picked up a discarded newspaper, folded it and placed it beneath the counter with the others. Actually, the argument had ended the moment he had reached out, touched her cheek and looked into her eyes. Her insides had melted and her anger had dissolved into a little puddle. The memory of his lips pressed against hers had flooded her being. She had insisted that he leave the restaurant, that she could handle the work load without his help.

"You would really have enjoyed how angry Bob Hampton was after his conversation with Trent."

"You seem to have raised your opinion of Trent. Now, if I could just get Mike to lighten up. He called a little while ago, says he'll be back to work tomorrow. I'm sure glad to hear that. Charlene came back this afternoon. Now maybe things can return to normal."

"I'll have a little talk with Mike. I think he's off base about Trent. You can't help but like a guy who can get the best of Bob Hampton." Jake's voice trailed off, his words more representative of his private thoughts than an attempt at conversation. "There's a lot of intelligence and savvy there and a very commanding presence." He quickly returned his thoughts to the moment at hand as he glanced at his watch. "Uh, oh. It's almost six o'clock. I've got to go."

Cassie's teasing grin conveyed itself in her words. "Where are you off to in such a rush? Big date?"

Jake's cheeks turned a bright red as he lowered his gaze. "Well, I did ask Anne if she'd like to watch a movie with me. I rented a video, a Fred Astaire and Ginger Rogers film. Anne really likes their movies."

She reached across the bar and gave his cheek a little pat. "Why you little devil, who would have guessed that you're really a closet romantic—Fred Astaire instead of John Wayne?"

He tried to appear irritated, an attempt that did not work at all. "Cut that out, Cassie. It's just a movie."

She smiled knowingly. "Of course."

Five

Trent sat on the porch swing, waiting for Cassie to close the bar for the night. He had reluctantly left the restaurant that morning at her insistence. He had missed seeing her during the day, missed hearing her voice, missed the feisty glint that would come into her eyes when she was irritated with him. He liked the way she stood up for herself, asserted her authority rather than deferring to the way he kept trying to take charge of things.

When he saw her emerge from the restaurant he left the porch and met her on the path. "I'll carry that for you." He took hold of the cash drawer and the bar checks as they walked into the house. He set everything on the table in her office then turned to her, placing his hands on her shoulders. He searched her face before settling his gaze on her bright hazel eyes.

Cassie felt her insides quiver. He had such a disconcerting effect on her. When he touched her, nothing in the world mattered except being with him. She did not understand it, but knew it was so. His voice was soft, a verbal caress. "Will Mike be back tomorrow?"

"Yes, he called this afternoon and said he was feeling much better and would be in for sure. Charlene got back this afternoon." Cassie was barely able to speak. She felt herself being drawn by the pull of his magnetic spell.

"Good." He laced their fingers together. "As soon as you close the restaurant tomorrow let's go on a picnic. It's supposed to be a beautiful day and I'd like to see more of the island. Besides, it would allow us to be away from your business situation." His voice took on a teasing quality. "Maybe we can spend some time together without anything to cause an argument."

She was totally mesmerized, caught up in the ethereal net he had thrown around her. "A picnic? But it would be going on three o'clock before we could even get started. We couldn't do that."

"Why not? One of the nice things about being this far north is that it stays light so long. It's not even June yet and look how late the daylight lingers." His tone of voice, once again, teased her. "Or do you have some sort of a rule about going on picnics with people who rent rooms from you?"

As she had done before where Trent was concerned, she threw caution to the wind. A picnic—being able to spend some leisurely time alone together. Yes, she would like that very much. She watched as Trent descended the stairs toward his room, then tried to still the tremors that coursed through her body as she went into her own bedroom and shut the door. Her fingertips touched her lips where his had enveloped her in a good-night kiss.

Cassie put the Closed sign in the restaurant window then quickly tended to the end-of-shift details. Twenty minutes later everything was done. There was nothing standing between them and the picnic.

She had collected one of the good bottles of wine from the bar, ignoring Mike's pointed glare of disapproval, and packed some chicken and a nice salad into a picnic basket. She had been surprised by Anne's cautious comment that perhaps she was rushing things too much with Trent, that she really did not know anything about him. She dismissed Anne's concerns in the same way she had dismissed Jake's concerns and Mike's disapproval. Perhaps she was throwing caution to the wind, but it was her choice. She simply could neither ignore nor quell the tremors of excitement Trent created in her.

Cassie drove them partway around the island, stopping at a grassy bluff overlooking the channel. Trent spread the picnic blanket on the ground under a tree and Cassie set down the picnic basket. "Come on," she said, grabbing his hand and giving a tug as she headed toward the edge of the bluff, "let's take a look." She released his hand and walked ahead of him.

Trent caught up to her and recaptured her hand, lacing their fingers together. "What are we looking for?"

"Whales. Killer whales—Orca. It's a little bit early but we might get lucky. When the salmon invade these waters, headed up river to spawn, the whales have a feast. It's their favorite food. It usually starts in June." She turned toward him. "Have you ever seen a killer whale?"

"No, at least not in the open ocean where they live."

Trent released her hand and put his arm around her shoulder, drawing her close to him. They stood in silence for fifteen minutes scanning the surface of the water. They did not see any whales, but they both became startlingly aware of their closeness and the lack of any outside influence to interrupt that togetherness. Without any words they both turned away from the bluff and returned to their picnic lunch.

Cassie set out plates and food while Trent opened the bottle of wine and poured each of them a glass. He raised his glass toward her. "To you." He looked longingly into her hazel eyes. "To a generous, gracious and beautiful woman who has been casting a spell over me from the moment we met. To a woman who has forced me to reconsider my life and think about changes." He saw a flush of embarrassment cover her cheeks at the same time that confusion came into her eyes. He should not have said what he did. He had revealed too much.

He held her gaze for a long moment, then softly caressed her cheek. His words were as soft as his touch. "I know you don't understand—I'm not sure I do, either." What he did understand was that he would not be leaving the island as casually as he had originally anticipated—if he left at all. He wanted to get a look at Cassie's lease, see exactly how things stood. He allowed a fleeting thought about checking into taking the Washington bar exam so he could practice law in the state and take care of his own legal transactions rather than relying on someone else to fill the role he was totally qualified for.

As quickly as the business thoughts entered his mind, he dismissed them. His thoughts, his feelings . . . his desires . . . were consumed by the nearness of Cassie Brockton and by his own growing passion for her.

They ate their food and drank their wine. Each pretended a casual air, the enjoyment of a simple picnic. They talked about safe topics—art, books, current events, music. He managed to sidestep her questions about his personal life, thankful that she had not pressed him for specific answers. Her smile was enchanting. Her laugh caused little chills of excitement to race down his spine.

She sensed his reluctance to talk about himself, to reveal any personal information, so she stayed away from any specific questions even though she desperately wanted to know everything about him. She wanted to know exactly who she was falling in love with.

And that was precisely what she was doing. She was falling in love with him. There was no use denying it. She had started falling in love with him one minute after she fell off the ladder and into his arms, and she had confirmed that feeling with their first kiss.

She allowed a thought as to his real feelings about her—was she just another woman, in a long line of many, that he had met on his wanderings and totally captivated with his charming manner, or did he really care for her? The words he had uttered earlier when he proposed the toast lingered in her mind. She wanted so much for them to be true.

Her thoughts were quickly lost to the sensual fire of his lips as he leaned his face into hers. All her doubts, concerns and apprehensions disappeared as she responded to his kiss, giving totally of her deep feelings for him.

They sat next to each other on the picnic blanket. It had been a delightful time—Trent felt very comfortable with Cassie, very content. He watched her as she talked, as she laughed. She was exactly what he had always wanted—an intelligent, independent woman totally without phony pretenses. He captured her mouth and then enfolded her in the warmth of his embrace. He twined his fingers in her hair, caressed her back and shoulders. He did not understand how she had become so important to his life, so important to him, in such a short period of time.

Could he be falling in love with her? Could he allow it to happen with this deception hanging between them? Could he allow it to happen knowing her feelings about his chosen profession? Could he allow it to happen knowing what he had planned and what he would be doing? He dismissed his concerns as he darted his tongue into the dark corners of her mouth, reveling in her delicious taste.

He slowly sank to the ground, pulling her with him. The late-afternoon sun warmed their skin, and a gentle breeze wafted across their bodies, tickling their senses with the clean ocean air. Loose tendrils of her hair fluttered across her face until he smoothed them out of the way. They were in a world of their own, apart from any other reality.

Trent was not sure how far to take the sensual heat that was building between them. Even though they were alone, they were still out in the open where anyone could wander by and see them. He did not want to cause her any concern or embarrass her but, on the other hand, he wanted much more of her than just the kisses they had shared—as delightful as they were.

Reluctantly he broke off the kiss and cradled her head against his shoulder as he held her in his arms. He felt her closeness as she lay stretched out next to him, her arm across his chest. He held her, gently caressing her cheek and stroking her hair. It was comfortable—she felt so right in his arms.

Cassie snuggled her head into his shoulder. Even through his shirt his taut, muscular chest caused tingles to ripple from her fingertips through her body. She wanted more of him, but this certainly was not the place to pursue those feelings. She closed her eyes, a smile curling the corners of her lips as she moved her hand across his chest and along the side of his neck before running her fingers through his thick blond hair.

They stayed together, wrapped in each other's arms, as the sun dipped toward the horizon and the breeze turned cool. Trent felt Cassie shiver. He pulled her closer to him, sharing his warmth as he spoke. "It's getting cool out here. If you shift your weight a little I can get the edge of the blanket wrapped around your shoulders."

"Actually—" she reluctantly wiggled out of his embrace "—it's probably time to start back." Their eyes met, and the incendiary look that passed between them was unmistakable. She felt the pull of his magnetism as she melted back into the warmth of his arms. The passion of his kiss again consumed her and inflamed her desires.

Dusk had settled around them before they finally gathered their picnic things and started back. Their conversation was light and casual. They spoke as old friends would—old friends who were very comfortable with each other.

Cassie made an appearance in the bar to check on Mike. She was surprised at the number of customers— Mike was dashing around like crazy trying to keep up with it all. She immediately took over waiting on the tables.

After fifteen minutes Trent became concerned when Cassie did not return to the house, and he wandered over to the bar to see if everything was okay. As soon as he saw what was going on he stepped in to help Mike behind the bar. He started by washing the backlog of dirty glasses, refilling the ice bins and icing down bottles of the most popular brands of beer. Mike did not say anything, but his expression showed that he was grateful for the volunteered help. Business stayed brisk until closing.

Cassie locked the door after the last customer, and put out the Closed sign. "Whew! That was quite a rush." She plopped down on a bar stool. "There should be some good totals on the register."

"Here." Trent handed her a glass of wine. "Sit down and relax for a minute." He grabbed a bottle of beer from the ice and held it up toward Mike. "How about you?" Trent opened it as Mike nodded his head in agreement while ringing out the totals on the register. Trent started to pour himself a glass of wine, then changed his mind. Instead he poured himself a draft beer in an attempt to create some kind of a common area with Mike.

"Thanks." Mike picked up the cold beer and took a long draw directly from the bottle. "That hits the spot." He handed the cash register tape to Cassie. "It was a good night's business."

Cassie suppressed the smile that tried to curl the corners of her mouth. It was very obvious to her that Jake had talked to Mike, as he had said he would. Mike was making a genuine effort to be friendly, or at least Mike's version of friendly, with Trent. Trent's gesture of having the beer rather than the wine did not escape her notice, either. Everything seemed to be so perfect. She did not even mind that Trent had made the decision to jump in and help without consulting her first.

She listened as the two men made an earnest attempt at friendly conversation. The topic they finally settled on was fishing. As they warmed to their discussion, Cassie went around the bar to the register to count out the cash drawer.

Trent saw the perplexed look on her face as she stared at the money piled on the bar, the bills neatly stacked and wrapped next to the coins. She went through them again, counting every last penny. The furrow in her brow deepened as she stared at the money.

"What's the matter, Cassie?" Trent circled around behind the bar and stood beside her. "Is something wrong?"

"The cash drawer is short." She lifted up the front of the drawer and looked under it where it fit into the register drawer. There was nothing there. "It's short by fifty dollars. That's quite a bit."

Mike was there immediately. "There's nothing under the cash drawer? I took in a fifty-dollar bill from Jim Spencer—he wanted change. I shoved it under the drawer just like I do with anything over a twenty, along with any checks and credit-card receipts." He shot a hard look at Trent, then returned his attention to Cassie. "Do you have any fifties there in the stacks?" He indicated the wrapped bills stacked on the bar.

"No, no fifties at all." She picked up the wrapped stacks of bills and sifted through them carefully, looking at the denomination of each bill, hoping she had stuck the fifty in with some other bills—but no luck. "Nope, no fifty."

Mike glared at Trent. "What happened to it?" There was no mistaking his meaning or his accusation.

"I never saw it, so I couldn't say." Trent glared back, not sure quite what to do. He understood Mike's suspicion falling on him, and he also felt that there was no reason to suspect Mike of having taken it . . . unless Mike was purposely attempting to discredit him.

Trent dismissed that thought as being too ridiculous to pursue—maybe back home but not here on the island. "It has to be here somewhere." Trent squatted down, looked under the bar and searched the surrounding floor area. "Maybe down here." He moved things around, looking behind bottles. But after a thorough search he came up empty-handed.

Again Mike glared at Trent, his accusation clear to everyone present, then he turned toward Cassie. "I know I shoved a fifty-dollar bill under the cash drawer. We were very busy and I was rushed, but there's no mistaking the denomination of the bill. It was a fifty and not a twenty."

Trent turned to Cassie, his voice and manner calm. "I can't explain what happened, but I can understand that you would automatically suspect me. After all, I am a stranger here. If it will settle this matter, even though I neither saw nor touched the fifty-dollar bill, I'll replace it." He held her gaze, his eyes showing open honesty.

She quickly stepped between the two men. "Cut it out, both of you. I'm not accusing anyone of stealing. There has to be another explanation, some logical reason for the fifty being gone. Now, I don't want to hear any more about it tonight." Her attitude was not angry, just very authoritative and businesslike. She made no accusations or excuses. "Mike, put the money back into the cash drawer and then take the drawer out of the register. Trent, make sure the front door is locked and turn out the lights. This bar is now closed."

Trent did as he was instructed, returning to the bar when he had finished. His analytical mind tried to sort out what had happened and what to do about it. The amount of money, fifty dollars, had no particular meaning to him—it was a small amount by his standards, a mere pittance. What was troublesome was the exchange of words that had just taken place and the tension that filled the air. The last thing Trent wanted was for Cassie to have doubts and concerns about his continued presence.

Mike lifted the front of the cash drawer and pressed the release that allowed it to be removed from the register drawer. He scowled as he tried it again. Something was wrong—the mechanism seemed to be jammed. He closed the register drawer and opened it again, then made another try at removing the inner cash drawer.

Cassie and Trent both became aware of Mike's struggle with the drawer. "What's the matter, Mike?" Cassie quickly moved toward the register.

"I don't know. The release seems to be caught on something. The drawer won't lift out." For five minutes Mike shoved, wiggled and tugged at the release and the cash drawer. After uttering a string of obscenities he felt the release finally give way, and the cash drawer slid out of the register drawer. He stood with the cash drawer in his hands, staring at the release mechanism at the back of the register drawer.

Mike set the cash drawer down on the bar, reached into the back of the register and withdrew a crumpled and torn piece of paper. He smoothed out the fifty-dollar bill and laid it on the bar.

Trent saw the embarrassment dart across Mike's face as Mike looked from Cassie to Trent then back to Cassie. Before Mike could say anything, Trent spoke up. "There...I knew there was some logical explanation for what happened. Now we can all call it a day and get some sleep."

Mike watched as Cassie's gaze met Trent's, her face openly displaying the tender feelings that coursed through her and his face reflecting those same feelings. Mike shifted his weight awkwardly as he tried to speak. "Look, uh, I guess I was a little hasty—"

"Good night, Mike." Trent cut off his words with an upbeat tone of voice and a friendly smile.

Both Cassie and Mike watched Trent leave, then she picked up the cash drawer as she eyed Mike. "Well?"

"Come on, Cassie." His expression was that of a child who had been caught in some mischief and was trying to make his mother think it was not really that bad. "What was I supposed to think?"

"You were supposed to think that there must be some logical explanation. Today was not the first time that Trent has handled the money since he arrived. It would be so easy for him to steal it before it was recorded on the register tape. He's not so stupid that he would steal from your register after the amount had been rung up." She stood patiently, waiting to see what Mike had to say.

"Yeah, I guess you're right. I suppose you want me to apologize to him?"

"You do whatever you think is right but, in case you didn't notice, Trent let you off the hook."

Mike allowed a slight grin. "Yeah, I noticed."

Cassie gave him an affectionate hug before turning to leave, indicating that all was forgiven. "Good night, Mike. See you tomorrow." She took the cash drawer and left through the back door, leaving him to finish locking up.

She paused at the foot of the staircase before going up to the office. The light coming from beneath Trent's door indicated he was still up. She rapped lightly on the door. After a moment the door opened, the light flooding into the darkened hallway.

She started to speak, but before she could say anything Trent reached out and ran his fingertips seductively across her cheek, then twined his fingers in her hair and drew her to him. With his other hand he took the cash drawer from her and set it on the nightstand by his bed. He enfolded her in his embrace, holding her against his body. He did not try to kiss her, just held her close—her warmth and her softness overwhelmed him.

The soft knock at his door had startled him. He had been just ready to climb into bed when he heard her. Memories of their picnic had been circulating through his mind, warming him and tickling his nerve endings.

The warmth and strength of his embrace titillated her senses. This was not what she had intended when she knocked on his door. She had intended to tell him that she was sorry about the incident over the fifty dollars. She had intended only to say a few words, then go up to her room. Her intentions had disappeared in a heartbeat . . . a very excited heartbeat.

She tried once again to speak—mustering all her self-control. ''I only wanted to apologize about the incident with the fifty dollars.'' Her words, muffled in his chest, seemed to be drowned out by the sound of his strong heartbeat.

His voice was soft, his words almost a caress. ''There's nothing to apologize for. It was an honest mistake and it's now forgotten.''

Reluctantly she pulled away from his warm embrace. ''Thank you. Now, I'd better get to sleep.'' She reached for the cash drawer, then turned and left his room, shutting the door behind her. Upstairs she quickly undressed and got into bed. It was late—she needed to sleep. Her mind floated off on a cloud, her thoughts centered on Trent Nichols, then her eyes grew heavy and she drifted into a blissful sleep.

Trent did not get to sleep quite so easily. His mind clouded over with his confusion. He wanted Cassie; he wanted her very much. He also wanted to be honest with her. If only he knew what the outcome of that honesty would be. If only there was some guarantee that it would not alienate her.

It was a little after ten-thirty the next morning before Trent made an appearance at the restaurant to have breakfast. No sooner had Cassie served his food than Mike entered. Rather than going directly to the bar, he slowly made his way to the booth where Trent was seated. He awkwardly shifted his weight from one foot to the other.

"Listen, uh, about yesterday—"

"Hey, don't worry about it, Mike. It's forgotten." Trent flashed him a sincere smile and returned his attention to his breakfast. Mike continued to watch him for a minute longer then went to the bar to start his shift. As much as he did not want it to be so, Mike was beginning to like Trent.

Trent had already put in a busy day and it was not even lunch time yet. As soon as he had showered and dressed, he had gone directly to Cassie's office with the intention of finding a copy of her lease agreement with Bob Hampton. His thoughts had been dominated by one thing—his plans for the future. He had searched through all her files and finally found it. He had quickly read the legal document. One particular section had caught his attention and he had carefully gone back over it.

He had allowed a smile of satisfaction to turn the corners of his mouth as he returned the lease to the proper file folder. He had been very pleased with what he found. There was no doubt in his mind that Cassie was unaware of the specific provisions of the lease. He felt fairly confident that Bob Hampton did not know, either. Had he known, his correspondence with Randall Davies would have been of a much different nature.

Next he had checked his post office box. The only mail had been some routine updates from his office, nothing important. He had located a pay phone and called Randall Davies. He now had the missing pieces to his puzzle and was ready to put his plan into action. He had told Randall what he needed and asked him to get started on it right away.

Trent lingered over breakfast, sharing quick bits of conversation with Cassie as she took care of other customers. She introduced him to Charlene, a pleasant woman in her forties. Following breakfast he settled himself into the porch swing, leaned back and let out a sigh of contentment. He felt very good about the business arrangements he and Randall had discussed—very good, indeed. Everything was falling into place nicely.

His gaze wandered across the horizon. The view was breathtaking. The open water was dotted with a myriad of forested islands—some inhabited, some privately owned and some devoid of human population. He felt so relaxed and comfortable, knowing that he had made the right decision in wanting to stay. He put his thoughts on hold as he watched Cassie walk up the path toward the house.

He motioned for her to join him on the swing. "Busy day?" As he moved over to make room for her to sit down, he took the cash drawer and the ledgers from her and set them on the porch.

"Busy enough, but not too bad. With Mike and Charlene both back, things have returned to a normal routine. What have you been up to?"

"I spent some time reading this morning and since breakfast I've just been sitting here enjoying the clean air and the beautiful view." His voice grew very soft, very sensual. "What do you plan to do with the rest of today?"

"I...I have office work to take care of. I need to place my supply orders for both the restaurant and the bar. This is also the day I do the payroll."

"I see." He slipped his hand along the side of her face, then twined his fingers in her short hair. His words were a mere whisper as he leaned his mouth close to her ear. "Could I entice you to join me right here this evening for a glass of wine?" His lips tickled the sensitive area behind her ear before tugging gently on her earlobe.

She arched her neck, exposing more skin to his tempting mouth. She closed her eyes and allowed the sensations of his nearness to wash over her. "Mmm...I wouldn't be surprised to find that you could entice me to do just about anything you wanted."

Six

The words were said. She had not meant to say them out loud, but she certainly meant every word she said. She very much wanted Trent Nichols to make love to her; she wanted to make love to him.

Cassie finally extricated herself from his tempting nearness and went to her office. Her senses were alive, tingling with excitement. Every time he touched her the same thing happened. She had never had anyone excite her the way he did. It took considerable effort to turn her mind to the task at hand.

Trent's mind was filled with thoughts of Cassie. Her words about readily agreeing to anything he wanted played over and over through his consciousness. He left the porch and wandered back to the bar. The dozen or so patrons were watching a baseball game on television. He took a seat at the bar, ordered a beer and half-heartedly watched the game while making occasional small talk with Mike, who seemed to be still trying to apologize.

Trent quickly lost interest in the baseball game. He picked up a copy of the local newspaper and scanned the real estate ads, marking several properties for sale—both business and residential.

Jake's good-natured laugh and friendly greeting filled the room as he came through the door. He immediately spotted Trent and took a seat next to him. He indicated the television. "What's the score and what inning are they in?"

Trent's embarrassed smile said it all. "I haven't the slightest idea." He placed the newspaper on the bar. "I guess I'm not really watching it."

When Jake was around, things seldom stayed quiet for long. In a matter of minutes he had the entire bar involved in a discussion about football. As Jake explained to Trent, "Baseball's boring, football's exciting."

The conversation quickly segued from sports to fishing, a topic the locals seemed to prefer. "Do you have any plans for tomorrow?" Jake asked. "Why don't you go out with me in the morning? Fishing's a great way to get to know someone. We'll do a little fishing and exchange opinions on how to run the world in a more efficient manner."

Trent considered Jake's offer for a moment. "I'd like that. Let's do it."

"Good. We'll meet for breakfast at five o'clock, then go from there." After finalizing arrangements for the next morning, Jake excused himself and left to do errands.

Forgetting all about the newspaper he had marked up, Trent left the bar. Mike picked up the newspaper after Trent had left, stared at the markings, then frowned in confusion as he folded it and placed it with the other papers. He found it very strange that Trent had been busying himself with the local real estate and business opportunities section. Second thoughts made him retrieve the newspaper from the recycling stack; he was not sure exactly why.

Trent wandered into the small town and walked the streets, finally arriving at a real estate office. He looked at the photographs and read the descriptions of the various properties for sale. He continued to explore the town, making note of the various types of business and which ones seemed to be seasonal as opposed to year-round.

He went into the bookstore and browsed for a while, then wandered into a combination art gallery and gift shop. This particular business caught his eye because the merchandise seemed to be of superior quality, rather than typical tourist trinkets and T-shirts. One painting, in particular, immediately captured his attention.

He thought back to the night he had carried Cassie up to her bedroom. He visualized the interior of the room. Unlike the rest of the house, it had a much more modern look about it. It also had a sensual feel, reflecting the woman who occupied it. The colors were soft, muted shades with an occasional splash of a particularly vivid hue to bring everything alive.

The color and feel of the painting exactly matched her bedroom. He wanted to buy the painting as a present for her, so he had the gallery hold it for him. Pleased with his find, he returned to Cassie's house.

Cassie sat on the porch swing. She had procured a good bottle of red wine from the bar and had opened it, letting it sit on the small table to breathe. Thoughts filled her head, thoughts prompted by something Mike had shown her. As soon as she had entered the bar to select the bottle of wine, Mike had pulled the newspaper from beneath the counter and handed it to her. She had looked at him questioningly, not understanding what significance the newspaper was supposed to have, and he had quickly explained that the markings were Trent's. She again furrowed her brow in concentration. Why would Trent be marking local businesses for sale?

It was all very perplexing. She did not understand what it meant, other than raising one more question about exactly who Trent Nichols really was and why he was on the island. Mike had made it a point to tell her, even though he had been wrong about the fifty-dollar bill, that he still did not trust Trent. Mike had even gone so far as to suggest that Trent might be a con man after her money. He was sure Trent was hiding something and that she should be more cautious around him, make sure he did not have access to her business records. Cassie had laughed it off. The idea of him being after her money was preposterous—she had no money.

She watched as Trent walked up the path from the street. Just the sight of him caused her growing love to well up inside her, shoving aside all doubts and concerns. As soon as he saw her he smiled and waved. She returned his wave and held up an empty wineglass. Trent hurried the few remaining steps.

"Is this ready to pour?" He picked up the bottle and one of the glasses.

"Yes, you're just in time." She watched as he poured them each a glass then set the bottle down. She accepted the glass he handed her, offering him a shy smile.

He held his glass up to her. "To you, Cassie. A lovely lady who fills my every thought." They both drank, their gazes locked in an incendiary moment.

They each made a valiant attempt to ignore the heated desires quickly building between them. He told her about his exploration of the town that afternoon and his fishing trip planned for the next morning with Jake. They sipped their wine and watched as the sky took on all the colors of a brilliant sunset. Dusk turned to dark as they continued to talk quietly, the porch swing seductively swaying back and forth.

She snuggled next to his body in the darkness, his arm holding her close to him. Her mind kept going back to the newspaper Mike had shown her, back to the question of why he would be checking on real estate and businesses for sale. A thought tried to brighten the uncertainty that had settled over her. Maybe he was looking for a means of supporting himself so he would be able to stay for good, to stay with her. He had never mentioned any type of a job or how he could afford to spend an indefinite period of time on the island without concern for returning to his home and his work.

Cassie's words were hesitant as she finally found the courage to voice her concerns. "Trent?"

He kissed her on the forehead. "Yes?"

"This afternoon . . . in the bar . . ."

He immediately became aware of her apprehension and uncertainty. His senses jumped to attention. "What's wrong, Cassie?"

She sat upright, removing herself from his all-too-tempting magnetic pull. "What do you do . . . for a living, I mean? Are you in real estate?"

Her question surprised him. "What makes you ask that?"

"Well . . ." She swallowed, trying to chase away the tightness in her throat. "This afternoon, in the bar, you marked several local businesses that were for sale. Is that why you're here? To..." She was almost afraid to say the words out loud. "To buy some local business?" She had not actually formulated her exact fears until that minute. What if he was on the island for the purpose of buying out Bob Hampton? Jake had said that it was obvious that the two men did not know each other, but that did not mean that Trent had no interest in buying the property from him. Her voice quavered and her body began to tremble. "Are you here to help Bob Hampton take my business away from me?"

He heard her words, he heard the fear and anxiety in her voice. How could he answer her question? He took a calming breath and closed his eyes for a minute, trying to compose his thoughts. "A friend of mine in Seattle was contacted by Bob Hampton. My friend thought Bob's letter sounded vague and suspicious so he asked me if I would mind stopping off and checking into the situation for him. As a result of my report, my friend decided that he did not want to involve himself in whatever Bob Hampton had in mind."

"Oh." She did not know what to think. "So, that's the only reason you're here?"

"No. That's the reason I came here, not the reason I stayed. I called my friend with the information he wanted the first day I was here." He cupped her face in his hands and searched the depths of her eyes. His voice was very soft, very sensual. "I stayed because I found a delightful woman that I wanted to get to know much better." He knew he had not told her everything, that he had purposely bent the truth but, until Randall Davies had finalized Trent's instructions, there was nothing else he could say—except one thing. "Cassie, I would never do anything to purposely hurt you. You're very important to me."

She heard his words. They touched her heart. She loved him—there was no doubt in her mind. She rose from the swing, her voice thick with her desires despite her words to the contrary. "It's getting late and we both have to be up early."

"I know." He walked with her to the front door and opened it so she could enter. "Good night, Cassie." His touch lingered against her cheek as he looked longingly into the depths of her eyes. He softly brushed his lips against hers with tender loving concern rather than passion, then turned and entered the house through the door into his bedroom. He wanted to make sure that appearances did not compromise Cassie's reputation.

Trent went to his room, quickly undressed and climbed into bed. His body ached with his desire for her. His need to answer her fears with only half truths bothered him. It was a tricky double-edged sword. He wanted to make love to her, openly and passionately. On the other side, he was not able to be honest with her about who he was or what his undeclared intentions were. He had given it a lot of thought, a whole new direction for his talents and energies. Too many things—problems, hopes, desires, new plans—circulated through his head. He shoved the thoughts away, all but one. He climbed out of bed, quietly ascended the stairs and knocked at Cassie's bedroom door.

Cassie felt the tremors begin in the pit of her stomach and radiate outward. She had made her decision. She only hoped she was not making a fool of herself. He had said he would never hurt her and she believed him. She undressed, quickly showered then prepared to go to Trent's room. She slipped into her robe, ran a brush through her hair, then checked her appearance in the mirror. Butterflies flitted about inside her stomach and her pulse raced.

The soft knock at her bedroom door startled her. She had already made her decision—she was about to go downstairs, to go to Trent. She was just reaching for the doorknob. She opened the door.

The dim light from her bedroom spilled out into the hallway, highlighting his taut body and handsome face. Her gaze met his in a long, heated moment as she stared into the smoldering blue intensity of his eyes, then she stepped aside. Her voice was soft but contained neither hesitation nor uncertainty. "Come in."

Trent grasped her hand as he entered her bedroom, then he pulled her into his embrace. He caressed her back and shoulders as he buried his face in her hair. He pulled back slightly and looked deeply into her eyes as he gently cupped her face in his hands. "I want to make love to you, Cassie. I want this very much."

Her voice held all the passion stored inside her. "So do I." No other words were spoken; no words needed to be spoken. She loved him. She could not explain it but she knew it was so. She felt his arms tighten around her, the heat of his intensity flooding her being. Her fingers caressed the taut muscles of his back and shoulders, and her lips lightly brushed across his bare shoulder then tickled against his chest.

His nimble fingers moved quickly to the sash tied at her waist. A moment later it dropped to the floor. He slowly ran his hands inside her robe as he bent his head to capture her mouth. Her skin was smooth as silk, and the heat of her passion warmed his fingers. He wrapped his arms around her, his fingers tickling across her bare back. Her nudity beneath the robe surprised and pleased him.

Cassie trembled with excitement as he slipped the robe off her shoulders and let it drop to the floor on top of the sash. His mouth captured hers, his tongue darting and twining seductively. The force of his masculinity overpowered her. She melted into his being, giving in to all the passion he stirred within her. She pressed the fullness of her breasts against his body as he cupped the perfect roundness of her bottom.

She slid her hands down his back, tucking them inside the elastic band of his briefs. She tugged, slowly lowering the briefs past his hips until she felt the hardened arousal of his passion spring free of the confining fabric. She had never before been so bold, so aggressive. But then, no one had ever excited her the way Trent did.

He released her just long enough to discard his briefs. He relished the sensation of her bare skin against his— her hardened nipples pressing against his chest, the length of her body radiating heat to his needs. With a very smooth maneuver he laid her back on the softness of the bed and stretched his body out next to hers.

Cassie's breathing was becoming very erratic, matching Trent's as it came in ragged puffs. He smoothed her hair back from her face as he again captured her mouth in a frenzy of heated passion. His fingers stroked the length of her body, tracing the outline of her hip then coming to rest on the fullness of her breast. He tempted and teased the puckered, hard nipple with his fingers, then with his tongue before taking the taut peak into the warmth of his mouth. She uttered little moans of pleasure as he gently suckled.

She ran her fingers through the thickness of his blond hair as she rubbed her foot along the edge of his bare calf. She had known making love with Trent would be every bit this wonderful, every bit this exciting. She caressed his shoulders and back, dipping her fingers occasionally to tickle across the skin of his bottom.

Her touch sent tremors of fire through his body. He knew he would not be satisfied until he had explored everything, intimately knew all of her. Her taste, her feel, the unselfish way she gave her warmth and herself—she was like an addictive substance. No matter how much he had, he wanted and needed more. His fingers slid smoothly up her inner thigh then danced through the downy curls nestled across her femininity.

As he quickly moved to suckle her other breast and his hands again stroked the smooth skin of her inner thighs, a delicious shudder shot through her body and settled low in the heated center of her being. She felt his fingers twirl through the downy softness between her thighs and this time slowly slip through the moist folds of her womanhood.

Her whimper of delight was cut off when his mouth came down hard on hers, his labored breathing matching her own. She had never before felt the level of excitement he created in her, experienced the all-consuming passion that coursed through her being at that moment.

He continued to titillate her body with his sensual mouth—tasting the softness of the valley nestled between her breasts, kissing her stomach, running his tongue around her navel and then moving to her abdomen. His hot breath came in short, ragged puffs as his lips teased the sensitive skin of her inner thighs, causing her to gasp sharply then let out a soft, sensual moan.

He found the hot core of her moist pleasure center, eliciting shudders and throaty gasps of unbridled passion as he tasted her delicate femininity. She arched toward him, demanding and receiving more of his sensual ministrations. Then, from deep inside her being, wave after wave of explosive ecstasy welled up and swept through her body, the surging tide continuing beyond her wildest expectations. Finally the waves subsided.

He gently cupped and caressed the fullness of her breasts, reveling in the silky feel of her skin. He provocatively ran his fingers through the downy softness of her triangle as he whispered in her ear. "I want to give you more pleasure again and again."

She ran her hands over his hard-muscled chest, tickling her fingers through the wisps of sandy-colored hair. Her hands lingered here and there as she bestowed little kisses and nibbles on his shoulders and across his chest. Her fingers reached down for his throbbing arousal, softly caressing and stroking his hardened need. She again lost herself to his delicious lovemaking—his bare skin against hers, the sensations she experienced from his electrifying touch.

Trent inserted his knee between her thighs as she opened herself to receive his pressing desire. He poised his body above hers then slowly penetrated the moist heat of her sex with his hardness as a low, throaty growl escaped his lips. He consumed the sweetness of her mouth as he set a slow, smooth rhythm. Their hips moved in perfect unison—they were so in sync, so attuned to the wants and needs of the other. His strokes increased in intensity; their thrusting accelerated. Their shared sensations built to a fever pitch, then their incendiary passions exploded.

His muscles tensed as she dug her fingers into the firm flesh of his bottom. A shudder moved through his body as he gave a final deep plunge. Time teetered on the brink of infinity as she gasped and joined him in delicious release.

They soared on the wings of ecstasy to the far edges of space as they abandoned themselves to wanton desires until both were completely spent. Their skin glistened with beads of perspiration, their arms and legs were tangled and their bodies exhausted. Their inner beings radiated the glow of their ethereal oneness. He brushed a loose tendril of hair from where it clung to the dampness of her cheek, then placed a soft kiss there as he enfolded her in his warm embrace.

Both lay quietly, enveloped in the warm cocoon that surrounded the afterglow of their lovemaking. Neither spoke, neither wanted to break the magical spell they were experiencing. Slowly their breathing returned to normal. Cassie rested her head against the dampness of his chest, the sound of his strong heartbeat filling her being with his nearness. He twined his fingers in her tawny hair while gently stroking down her back and across her bottom.

Cassie closed her eyes as she snuggled her body next to his. She had never before felt so euphoric, so content, so happy... so in love. She drifted into a blissful sleep.

Trent did not have quite as easy a time of it. There were so many things he wanted to say to her, so many feelings and emotions he wanted to share. Most of all, he wanted to be honest with her. He did not want any deceptions to stand in the way of his growing love for her.

He looked at her as she lay sleeping in his arms. He was digging himself deeper and deeper into a hole. He had to figure some way of getting out of it without losing her. He placed a tender kiss on her forehead, gently pulled her closer to him and closed his eyes.

Trent woke with a start as the cold air hit his skin where just moments before Cassie had nestled next to him. He reached out and grabbed her wrist, pulling her next to him as she tried to quietly slip out of bed. In a voice thick with sleep he asked, "What time is it?"

"It's four in the morning. I'm opening up instead of Charlene and I have to be at work in forty-five minutes." The warmth of his touch as he grasped her wrist sent tingles through her body.

He focused on her as the fuzziness of sleep cleared from his head. "You can spare five minutes." He enfolded her in his embrace, all the tender feelings and heated passions of the night before surging through his being.

All her desires were instantly rekindled the moment she felt his fingers wrap around her wrist and heard his thick, sleepy words. A shiver darted up her spine when his tongue teased her nipple to a taut peak. "I don't have five...mmm...well, no more than five minutes." Her breathing quickened, her eyes closed and a smile curled the corners of her mouth. She wrapped her arms around his neck and ran her fingers through his thick, tousled hair as she rubbed her foot against his leg.

She had to put a stop to this all-too-tempting seduction he had started. She had to get ready for work. She had to...she did not know what it was she had to do, she only knew that he totally clouded her better judgment so that she could not think straight.

She was so exquisite, so delightful, so open and honest in her response. Everything about her excited him. He liked touching her, feeling the silkiness of her skin, kissing her and now he could add making love to her to that list. He also liked talking to her—just being with her.

He nuzzled her neck as he rolled her over on top of him, holding her tightly. They both lay quietly for a moment longer, his arms wrapped around her and her head resting against his chest. It was Cassie who broke their moment of reverie. "As delightful as this is, if I don't get out of this bed right now I'll be late."

Reluctantly Trent released her from his embrace. He kissed her on the cheek, then allowed her to slip out of bed as he climbed out after her. "We both have to get moving. I'm meeting Jake at five o'clock."

Cassie picked up her robe from the floor then turned toward the bathroom. She felt his touch on her arm, bringing her to a halt. She turned and looked into his troubled blue eyes. He was not able to hide the quick look that darted through them. "Trent? What's wrong?"

"Cassie..." He gently caressed her cheek with his fingertips as he continued to gaze into the depths of her hazel eyes. "There's so many things I need to..." He quickly wrapped his arms around her and drew her to him, burying his face in her hair in order to stop his own words. This was not the time. He could not just blurt it out. He had to carefully choose his words so that she would understand—so that she would not be hurt or angry over his deception, over what he planned to do, over the direction he planned to be moving in the very near future. He pulled back from her, his face masking his true emotions. "It's getting late."

"Good morning, Jake." Cassie filled his cup with freshly brewed coffee.

"Hi, Cassie." Jake looked around the deserted restaurant. As usual, he had been waiting when she unlocked the door to open for business. "Where's Trent? We're going fishing today. He's supposed to meet me here."

"I'm sure he'll be along any minute. I heard his shower running when I left this morning."

"Good morning, everyone." Trent's voice came from the kitchen as he made his way to the front of the restaurant.

Jake watched with keen interest, first noting that Trent had used the back entrance rather than the front door that was for customers, and second seeing the way Cassie and Trent looked at each other—their gaze locked together in a moment so intensely hot that he could almost feel the heat of their all-too-obvious passion for each other. Both were totally oblivious of anything and everything surrounding them. It lasted for only a moment but it was long enough for Jake to form some very definite opinions.

Breakfast was quick. As the two men rose to leave, Cassie pulled an envelope out of the cash register and handed it to Trent. "Here, this is for you."

He took the envelope from her, confusion covering his face. He opened it and stared at the check then looked back at her. "What's this?"

"It's a paycheck, for the day you worked in the bar when Mike was sick."

He quickly grabbed her arm and pulled her aside, out of earshot from anyone who might be listening. "You didn't tell me to work—I volunteered my help. You're not obligated to pay me for those hours. You can't afford to be doing that." Again he had taken charge of things, making her decisions for her.

She reached her fingers to the corners of his mouth and turned them up into a smile, then smoothed out the furrow on his brow. "Watch your posterior. You're about to get that swift kick in the seat of the pants. Once again you seem to have forgotten that I'm the owner of this business. You worked the hours and you should be paid for them."

She flashed him a sly grin. "Jake's waiting. You'd better get going. He firmly believes that if the boat isn't where he wants it before seven in the morning the fish will refuse to bite."

He tried to muster a stern look, while at the same time lovingly caressing her cheek with his fingertips. "We'll discuss this tonight."

Trent had a much better day than he had anticipated. Fishing was not really one of his favorite things. To his surprise he found that his day with Jake consisted of very little fishing and a great deal of interesting conversation combined with a sight-seeing tour around the islands.

When Trent had first approached Jake's boat it had appeared, from a distance, to be battered and dirty, but once aboard he found it to be neat and remarkably clean for a commercial fishing boat. Everything was orderly, and the installed equipment included the latest in sonar, radar and radio gear.

Trent felt very comfortable with Jake. He was surprised at the wide variety of knowledge Jake possessed. They discussed many topics, exchanging intelligent information and opinions. They took a seagoing tour around the islands, with Jake pointing out the sights and providing interesting tidbits of local history.

In late morning Jake swung the boat around and headed back toward home. He navigated out into the main channel, the water immediately becoming very choppy due to the large oceangoing vessels using the passageway. "Whoa! We must be at the middle of rush-hour traffic. This is the choppiest I've ever seen these waters without the help of bad weather." The thirty-foot boat was buffeted about with increasing regularity as they moved farther out into the main channel. A sudden thud jolted the fishing boat, sending Trent sprawling to the deck as he tried to grab hold of anything to maintain his balance. Jake was not as lucky. He was thrown hard against the open hatch door of the hold.

Trent quickly regained his footing. Jake, however, was not so quick to get to his feet. He grabbed his left leg and grimaced in pain. "I think I've broken it."

Without a wasted minute Trent immediately took control of the situation. "Don't move. Keep your leg immobile. Do you think you can hang on until I get us out of the middle of this channel?"

Jake shot him a dubious look. "Do you think you can handle her okay?"

His question was answered with a confident smile. "No problem. You just try and relax."

Jake watched, amazed, as Trent took the controls of the fishing boat and handled them with expert efficiency, including placing a radio call to have medical help waiting at the harbor when they arrived. As he pulled around the bend and came in sight of the dock he radioed the harbormaster and confirmed that the emergency medical van was waiting.

Trent maneuvered the boat into a temporary tie-up position at the pier without any difficulty, then tossed a bow line and stern line to the dockhand, who quickly secured them. He stood aside as the medical technicians came aboard and took Jake off the boat.

As Jake was being carried from the boat, the harbormaster came up to Trent and spoke in hushed tones. "Uh, Mr. Nichols, this isn't Jake's docking space. This is only for temporary docking. If the boat stays here more than an hour I'll have to charge—"

The rest of the sentence was cut off by a harsh look from Trent and a sharp reply, his tone of voice clearly indicating his dominance of the situation. "If there's a problem, put it on my bill." Trent looked back toward Jake just in time to see his head snap to attention at Trent's words. There was no mistaking the surprised and curious look on Jake's face, the silent question in his eyes.

Trent accompanied them to the emergency medical clinic. He made no mention of the incident and Jake asked no questions. It was almost three hours before Jake's leg was tended to and he had been taken home. It turned out that the bone was only cracked, not broken. Trent made sure Jake was settled in and comfortable, then made a quick trip to the drugstore to fill Jake's prescription. Next he moved the fishing boat to Jake's proper docking space and secured it.

Glancing at his watch, Trent decided he had just enough time to get to the gallery and pick up the painting he had put on layaway. He wanted to get it back to Cassie's house and hang it in her bedroom before she closed the restaurant and went back to her office.

Seven

Trent sat on the edge of Cassie's bed absorbing the overall effect the painting had on the bedroom. He liked it; he liked it very much. He hoped she would, too. He placed a card on her dresser, then left the bedroom.

He returned to his room, removed an envelope from the dresser drawer and placed the check she had given him inside it, along with all the tip money he had accumulated that same day. He planned to give her the tip money, as well as return the paycheck.

He heard Cassie enter the house and go upstairs. Moments later he was jarred to attention by the sound of someone charging down the stairs, then banging loudly on his door. He smiled to himself as he went to answer her knock.

His teasing smile and twinkling blue eyes greeted her as he opened the door. "That's an awful lot of noise for just one little girl. What seems to be the problem?"

"The problem?" Her voice vacillated between mere excitement and overwhelming joy. "The problem, Trent Nichols, is the painting that's hanging on my bedroom wall!"

He mimicked her excited tone. "Well, Cassie Brockton, what about the painting that's hanging on your bedroom wall? Is there something wrong with it?" It took all his willpower to keep from grabbing her in his arms and smothering her with thousands of kisses.

She threw her arms around his neck, the total elation she felt at that moment radiated from her face and filled the room. "It's beautiful. I love it."

He grabbed her to him and, with his arms wrapped around her, lifted her off the floor and swung her around as they both laughed and enjoyed their closeness. "I'm glad you like it."

"I don't just like it, I love it, but it's far too expensive a gift...."

He set her back down on the floor but continued to hold her tight against his body. His teasing words tickled across her ear. "Didn't anyone ever tell you that it's not polite to discuss the cost of a gift?" He kissed the tender skin behind her ear as he twined his fingers in her hair.

She pulled back slightly, her gaze searching the depths of his eyes. "I love it so much, but I can't accept it. It's much too expensive a present."

"No, it isn't. In fact, it isn't anywhere near what I would like to have done. The second I saw that painting I knew it would be perfect on your wall."

"I don't know what to say." Her words were soft, her feeling of joy filling her inner being. She rested her head against his chest, her arms circling his waist.

She had been shocked when she entered her bedroom and had seen the painting hanging over the dresser. She had stood perfectly still for the longest moment just staring at it, her mind confused about where it had come from. Then she had seen the card on the dresser. With trembling fingers she had removed it from the envelope. *"A beautiful painting to enrich the surroundings of the beautiful lady who has enriched my life. Trent."*

He held her close, caressing her back and shoulders. "I'm glad you like the painting." They remained in each other's arms, quietly enjoying the moment of tender caring.

After several quiet minutes she raised her head from his chest and looked into the sky blue depths of his eyes. "You make me feel so very special."

"You are very special." He cupped her chin in his hand, tilted her head and softly covered her mouth with his in a gentle and caring kiss.

The bar business was brisk but not so hectic that Trent had any problems handling it by himself. Besides, it would be only for a couple of hours. Cassie had gone to Jake's house to see how he was doing and to check on whether he needed anything. Trent had been able to tell that Mike wanted to go with her, so he had volunteered to take care of the bar for a while.

Bits and pieces of conversation drifted in his direction, conversation that bothered him. People were speculating about the California-registered yacht out of Marina Del Rey that had been docked in the harbor for the past several days. No one had been seen aboard, and the harbormaster was not willing to provide any information about it. The mysterious yacht was quickly becoming a popular topic of conversation among the locals.

He wondered if Jake would say something to Cassie or Mike about the quick conversation he had overheard between the harbormaster and Trent. His brow furrowed slightly as he wondered if he should ask for Jake's discretion or hope that it would just drop and be forgotten.

Cassie and Mike returned to the bar. Both seemed relieved that Jake's condition was not very serious. He would be up and around with the aid of a crutch and should be totally unencumbered in a few short weeks. Mike took back his bartending duties.

It was still early. Trent asked Cassie if she would like to go for a walk with him. They walked through town and then along the harbor, holding hands as they strolled. He felt so comfortable with her, so relaxed and unpressured. Life on the island seemed truly idyllic, an answer to his quest.

She thrilled to his touch as he took her hand, not caring who saw them or what they thought. His warmth spread to her as he laced their fingers together. She felt so free, so open. Every hour of every day he was becoming more and more the center of her universe. Her mind drifted to the night before, when they had made love. She had never had anyone make love to her with the degree of sensuality he possessed. The excitement still tingled through her body.

"There's the boat everyone's talking about." As they walked along the harbor she pointed to the spot where Trent's yacht was docked. "It's from California, but no one seems to know who it belongs to. It just arrived one day and no one's been seen on it. It looks like a very expensive boat. You'd think someone would be using it."

"Maybe the owner is visiting someone on one of the islands and this was the most convenient place he could find to leave it." He wanted to change the subject as quickly as he could. "This Monday, when you're closed—do you have any plans for the day?"

"Other than being able to sleep in until at least eight o'clock in the morning, nothing special."

"Good. Do you suppose I could prevail upon you to give me a tour of the island? Jake gave me an ocean going tour, but now I'd like a land tour."

"I'd love to."

"Then it's a date?" The adoration he felt for her emanated from the sky blue depths of his eyes as he squeezed her hand.

She felt a flush cover her cheeks and her insides tremble. Her voice was soft. "Yes, it's a date."

They slowly made their way back to her house. Trent was relieved that she made no mention of what Jake had overheard. Apparently Jake had forgotten or attached no significance to the exchange of words.

He walked her to the front door of the house, then after she entered he turned and went through his own door into his bedroom. He quickly moved through his room to the door leading to the rest of the house.

Stepping into the hallway, he called her name. Receiving no answer, he ascended the stairs toward the light. Perhaps she was in her office, absorbed in some business matter. When he reached the top of the stairs he immediately spotted her sitting on the edge of her bed, staring at the painting. A soft smile turned the corners of his mouth as he watched the glow of happiness radiating from her face. He stepped through the door and to her side.

Without actually turning to look at him, Cassie became aware of his presence. Her eyes never left the painting as she spoke to him in hushed tones—hushed, yet conveying her enthusiasm. "It's such a beautiful painting. I can't believe it's really mine. It has the look and feel of a Monet." She turned her head toward him, her hazel eyes soft with the depth of her emotion. "Don't you think so?"

He sat next to her, wrapped her in his embrace and pulled her to him. "Yes, I think so. The colors first attracted me, then it was the resemblance to Monet that kept my attention. You said he was your favorite artist."

She rested her head against his shoulder and let out a sigh. "You really shouldn't have done it. I feel very guilty about keeping it, but at the same time I couldn't bear to part with it."

"There's no reason for you to feel guilty. I bought it for you because I wanted you to have it." He kissed her tenderly on the cheek.

"Trent?" She looked up at him, her eyes capturing his gaze and her words tentative. "You didn't do this because of last night, did you? I mean...you didn't feel that you were obligated—"

"This has nothing to do with last night. If it would put your mind at ease, I'll let you in on a little secret. I had the gallery owner put it away for me yesterday afternoon."

She again rested her head against his shoulder and closed her eyes. A smile of utter contentment curled the corners of her mouth.

Time flew by for both Trent and Cassie, flew by almost too quickly. A foreboding would occasionally come over her. Trent had made no mention of his future plans. How much longer could he stay on the island? When would he have to leave, go back to his home? Where was his home? She loved him so much she knew she would just die if he left, but she did not know what to do to prevent it.

Evening faded into night as the sunset gave way to a black sky filled with a million twinkling stars. They sat on the porch swing enjoying a glass of wine. He was feeling a little uneasy about what was on his mind, what he needed to say. "Cassie..." Trent's voice and hesitation conveyed his nervousness. "I, uh, have some pressing matters that need to be tended to. Tomorrow morning I'll be taking the ferry to the mainland. I'll be back in two days."

She seemed very surprised, almost at a loss for words. "Pressing business? What...of course." Tremors of anxiety darted through her. She was so afraid that he was preparing to leave the island, making arrangements for a future that would not include her.

She had been dreading the time when he would actually leave. Maybe if she told him how she felt, told him that she loved him. Maybe that would make a difference, maybe then he would stay. She shook her head, a slight frown wrinkling her brow. No, that would be a bad idea. She wanted him to stay because he wanted to, not because he felt obligated in some way. She did not want to scare him off by making him think she was demanding some sort of commitment.

"That's an odd expression." He reached out and gently smoothed the frown lines across her brow. "Is there something wrong?"

She quickly recovered her composure. "No, of course not." She offered him a shy smile. "It's just that I'll miss you, that's all."

Under cover of the darkness of night, as they sat on the porch swing, he pulled her to him and covered her mouth with a soft, caring kiss. "I'm going to miss you, too." He took a calming breath while twining his fingers in her hair. "In fact, I'm going to miss you more than I thought it was possible to miss someone. Cassie, I . . ." He could not finish his sentence. He could not tell her how he really felt about her, could not say the words. He could not tell her that his feelings had moved far beyond just passion and desire, that he was definitely falling in love with her.

At least, not yet, not with the deception still hanging over his head. The deception again—he had to clear it up. He had to be completely honest with her. He had spent many hours agonizing over it—how to tell her, how to make her understand without hurting her or embarrassing her. Or more importantly, without driving her away from him. He also had to make her understand the master plan he was about to put into play, what he intended to do and why.

It was getting late and Cassie had to be up early. They went inside the house. She paused by his room before climbing the stairs, and he pulled her into his arms and lowered his head to hers.

The alarm jarred both of them awake at six o'clock. Trent reached to the nightstand and groped for the Off switch. Cassie rolled over and snuggled her body next to his warmth. He spoke in a voice still thick with sleep. "I'll work for you. That way you can sleep a little longer."

Her voice was equally filled with the lingering effects of sleep. "No, you won't." With a sly smirk she reached around and gave him a playful slap on his bare bottom.

With surprising swiftness he grabbed her wrist. "What was that all about?"

"It's still my restaurant. So, unless you're planning to steal it out from under me, I'm the boss and I make the decisions." She was too warm and contented to notice the quick look of anxiety that darted across his face. "You may consider that to be the equivalent of a swift kick to the seat of your pants."

His voice teased. "That's not quite accurate."

"What? Are you telling me I'm no longer the owner and operator of my own business?"

A quick frown darted across his face, then just as quickly disappeared. "That's not what I'm saying at all. It's just that—" he grinned mischievously at her "—in case you haven't noticed, I'm not wearing any pants."

Her eyes reflected the still-smoldering passions from the previous night's lovemaking. She brushed her fingertips softly across his thigh. "Trust me, I noticed."

His voice took on a husky quality as he again grabbed her hand and pulled it away from his body. "You do that again and neither one of us will be working at the restaurant this morning."

"Mmm...that's a delightful idea but not very practical." She placed a light kiss on his chest.

A thoughtful expression crossed his countenance. "Sometimes you simply have to cut loose and do what pleases you rather than always being practical." He spoke more to himself than to her. "Sometimes being practical isn't what's best. Sometimes it's hard to tell what's best."

She looked questioningly at him. Once again she did not understand exactly what he was talking about but knew it was something that came from inside him. She kissed him on the chest again, then slipped out of bed.

Trent boarded the ferry for the mainland. As soon as it docked he picked up the rental car he had arranged in advance and drove to Seattle. He immediately checked in to a tower suite at the Sheraton. He was pleased to see the garment bag hanging in the closet, the garment bag he had had his secretary ship from Los Angeles to coincide with his arrival. He glanced at his watch. He had just enough time to get a much-needed haircut.

Afterward he returned to the suite, quickly showered and changed into a business suit. His meeting was in fifteen minutes—he had cut his time very close.

Ten minutes later Trent responded to a knock on the door, admitting his visitor to the suite. He extended his hand. "How are you doing, Randall?"

"Thanks to you and your impossible time schedule, I've been busier than I would have liked. I even had to cancel my golf game yesterday."

For the next three hours the two men discussed the details of Trent's business project. When they had concluded their meeting they went to the hotel's dining room and had dinner. They agreed to meet at Randall's office the next day right after lunch. Randall's secretary would have most of the paperwork done by then. After that, there were numerous financial details to arrange. Tomorrow would be a very busy day. He needed to be fully rested.

Cassie had become so accustomed to having Trent around that she felt lost without him. She missed sitting in the living room as they watched television together, enjoying a glass of wine in the evening on the porch swing. She missed his cheery greeting to everyone—even missed the way he kept slipping into that authority mode of his and trying to take charge and run her business for her.

But most of all she missed their intimate time together. She missed the feel of his bare skin next to hers, the warmth of his body, the way he caressed her, the provocative combination of the tenderness of his touch and the heat of his passion. And, just as much, she missed the moments following their lovemaking when they would talk quietly together. She knew there were so many things she did not know about him, so much that he seemed to be hiding.

That thought brought her back to the here and now. He was due to return in the morning. Her eyelids grew heavy as she wondered what kind of pressing business he had on the mainland and where he had gone. She finally drifted off to sleep, her dreams filled with Trent Nichols.

"When is Trent coming back?" Jake sipped his coffee as he shoved his empty breakfast plate across the counter. "Not that it's any of my business—" his grin teased her "—but you've been moping around here like a little lost puppy since he's been gone." His face took on a caring look, the concern of a dear friend. "Are things as serious between you two as I think they are?"

A thoughtful look crossed her face, then she quickly covered it with a friendly smile. "He'll be back sometime this morning."

He eyed Cassie carefully. "That's only one answer. I asked two questions. Do you think, I mean, this has all happened very quickly. Maybe you should slow down a little in this thing with Trent. I like Trent, he's certainly a very personable guy, but things just don't add up." He paused as he looked thoughtfully into Cassie's hazel eyes. "Please don't take what I'm about to say in the wrong light. It's just that I care about you and don't want to see you get hurt by some charming stranger who's just passing through."

She looked at him curiously. "Jake, we've been very close friends from the moment I arrived on the island. I couldn't feel closer to you if you were my own father. I know you wouldn't do anything or say anything you didn't really believe." She saw the concern on his face. Tremors of anxiety started deep in the pit of her stomach. She was not at all sure she really wanted to hear what he was about to tell her.

"Cassie, honey." The words were difficult for him. "I think it might be a good idea for you to have Trent checked out—you know, hire a private investigator or something like that." He swallowed nervously, then continued with his thoughts. "I know how you feel about lawyers, but perhaps it would be a good idea if you contacted—"

The quick anger that flashed through her eyes said it all. "I'm surprised at you, Jake. What has Trent done to make you so suspicious?"

"It's nothing big or even anything specific. It's just lots of little things that by themselves don't really mean anything, but when you put them all together, well, please be careful. I don't want to see you hurt."

"You worry too much." She poured him some more coffee, gave him a warm pat on the cheek and a confident smile, then turned to the other customers. Jake's words, even though they were not what she wanted to hear, stayed with her. She knew—deep inside her being she knew—Trent was not being honest with her. She prayed she was not in over her head, that she was not so blindly in love with him that she was refusing to acknowledge what the probable truth might be.

The morning seemed to drag by. Jake's comments kept circulating through her mind. Sometimes it felt as if hours had passed but when she glanced at the clock she found it had been only fifteen minutes. Then, finally, she saw the ferry pull into the dock—the ferry that should be bringing Trent back to her.

All her doubts and concerns disappeared. She held her breath, and tremors coursed through her body. She watched as the passengers disembarked, watched the front walk from the dock to the restaurant. She did not see him. Had she missed him? Had he gone directly to his room first? Or—her greater fear—maybe he had not been on the ferry.

The restaurant was empty except for one lingering customer at the counter. Cassie sat in a corner booth and tried to compose her sinking feeling. He had to come back—he had personal belongings in his room. She waited. Another fifteen minutes passed. With a heavy heart she went about mechanically preparing for the lunch crowd.

Trent was furious. He was running behind schedule, with too many things to take care of and too little time. He was only five miles from the mainland ferry dock—cutting it very close, but he would just make it. Then it happened—a rear tire blew out. By the time he changed the flat and returned the rental car, the ferry had already set out for the island.

He stood on the dock, watching as the ferry disappeared over the horizon. It would be three hours before the next one departed for the island. He went into the coffee shop at the terminal building, found a seat and he thought about everything he had accomplished in Seattle. He felt very confident about his business dealings with Randall Davies; he was sure there would be no problems. All facets of his overall plan were now in motion. Soon all the pieces would come together. He was very anxious to see Cassie again. It felt like weeks since he had seen her, not two days.

The next two and a half hours passed very slowly for Cassie. Finally it was two o'clock. She put out the Closed sign, tended to the end-of-shift details, then went home. Once inside her house she closed her eyes and tried to compose her sinking feeling—where was Trent?

She needed to get her mind off her nagging fear. She went up to her office and opened a catalog to the page she had marked. When she had seen the wall plaques advertised she had thought they would be perfect for the bar, and she had been thinking about it for a few days. Now she had finally made up her mind. She filled out the order blank, wrote a check, addressed the envelope to the company in Los Angeles and mailed it. She had paid the additional amount to have them shipped air, and according to the ad the plaques would arrive in only ten days. She was anxious to hang them.

She heard the door open, then heard him come up the stairs as he called her name. Her heart did flip-flops. He was back. He was late but he had come back. She composed her elation, tried to bring her soaring excitement under control.

Trent was gorgeous. She immediately noticed his haircut, but it was more than that. Something was different—something about his look, his expression, his demeanor. She saw fires of excitement burning in his blue eyes.

He wrapped her in his embrace. "I'm sorry I'm late." His words teased; his lips brushed across her ear. "My belongings weren't scattered on the front porch. Does that mean I still have my room?"

Her words were a mere whisper. "Another five minutes and it would have been questionable." She wanted to know so many things but she was so thrilled to be back in his arms that nothing else mattered. All thoughts were lost as he covered her mouth with his, his kiss conveying a feeling of soft caring and at the same time the heated passion that coursed through him.

He pulled his face back from hers just enough to look into her eyes. His voice carried a hint of huskiness. He cupped her face in his hands and again brushed his lips against hers. A groan escaped his throat as he impulsively pulled her tightly against his body. "Oh, God, Cassie, I really missed you."

Her words were soft as she slipped her arms around his waist and laid her head against his chest. "I missed you, too, very much."

They stood quietly in each other's embrace, enjoying the feeling of closeness. Both felt the strong pull growing between them, the hunger that existed.

Trent smoothed her mussed hair away from her face as he placed a soft kiss on her forehead. Their lovemaking had been very intense. It had been only two days, but he felt as if he had been away from her for weeks. She had given his life such purpose, such meaning—more than he ever thought was possible.

He had almost told her of his plans and his feelings as they drifted in the warm afterglow of their union. He could not do it, though, could not offer her a commitment until he could share the complete truth with her. He could not ask her for a commitment based on a deception. His excitement over the wheels he had set in motion in Seattle was tempered with caution and uncertainty about her reactions.

Another two weeks at the most and everything would be put right. He had already committed a great deal of money to the project. The first phase of his plan had already been completed, and phase two was well under way. As soon as phase two was finalized, everything could be brought out into the open and all deceptions put aside.

Eight

The hours stretched into days and the days stretched into a week. Other than the fact that he ate breakfast at the restaurant, she did not know what he did with his time while she was working, but he always appeared as soon as she was finished for the day. The afternoons and evenings were always spent together—talking, watching some television in the evening, sometimes just sitting on the porch swing in silence while simply enjoying their closeness.

Cassie felt the air of excitement that surrounded him. She was acutely aware of the elation that bubbled inside him, that threatened to burst forth at a moment's notice. She had tried to subtly question him about it without seeming to be blatantly prying into his personal business, but each time he would just give her an inscrutable smile that widened into a Cheshire-cat grin and tell her that all things happen in their own good time.

She knew whatever had him so excited was connected with his trip to the mainland, but she simply could not imagine what it was. She finally gave up trying to pry the information out of him. She knew he would tell her when he was ready. It was funny—she felt so close to him, felt she knew him so well, even though she still knew so little about him. It was a strange paradox. Strange indeed.

"How's the leg doing, Jake?" Trent sipped his coffee as he sat next to Jake at the counter. "I see you've given up the crutch."

"Oh, it's doing just fine." He slapped his thigh and let loose with one of his jovial chuckles. "It's going to take more than a little tumble to keep me down." His expression turned serious. "I really appreciate you taking care of me like that. I suppose if I had been out there all alone I would have found some way of getting back to the dock, but it sure wouldn't have been easy."

Trent allowed a teasing anger. "If you don't stop telling me how much you appreciate me I'm going to stop talking to you. Enough, already!"

Jake became cautiously thoughtful. He carefully measured his words as he leveled a steady look at Trent. "All right. Is it okay if I tell you how impressed I was with your handling of my boat?"

An uncomfortable feeling welled up inside Trent. Enough time had passed since that day to allow him a sense of security. Jake had not mentioned the exchange of words he had overheard nor mentioned Trent's obvious expertise in handling the boat. He had thought the jeopardy had passed, that there would be nothing to explain. Now he was not sure.

He tried to toss the incident away as something that was not important. "I just got lucky."

Jake would not be put off. "No, that wasn't luck. You handled it with all the expertise of an experienced seaman." He took a steadying breath while looking around to see if Cassie was within earshot. He leaned forward and lowered his voice. "Several things have been running through my mind, more than just your handling of my boat and the hushed exchange of words between you and the harbormaster."

Trent's uncomfortable feeling was now bordering on anxiety. Apparently Jake had not discussed his thoughts with Cassie, but neither had he dismissed them from his mind. He wondered why Jake was bringing them up now. He tried to project a casual air. "There's no mystery. I've done a turn or two on a boat in my time."

"You've been on the island for quite a while without any visible means of support. How much longer do you plan to stay? Do you intend to walk away from here as casually and unencumbered as you arrived?"

Trent shifted uncomfortably on the counter stool and took a steadying breath. What Jake was asking was actually none of his business. Had they been in Beverly Hills he would have made that fact very clear. But, they were not in Beverly Hills. He knew Jake's motives were not malicious or devious in any way. He owed Jake the courtesy of an honest reply, as much so as possible.

Before he could answer, Jake continued. "I know it's none of my business, whatever it is that's going on between you and Cassie. But that girl's like the daughter I never had. I don't want to see her hurt by some charming drifter who's just passing through. You're hiding something, Trent. I don't know what it is and you certainly don't owe me any explanations but, if Cassie means anything to you at all, don't you think you should level with her?"

Trent stood and leaned forward, a pensive expression on his face, his head bowed in thought and his palms pressed flat against the counter. He knew he had been living on borrowed time, knew there was a very real possibility that someone would directly confront him and ask for some real answers. Things were so close. All the pieces would soon be together and the puzzle would be a complete picture—just another week or so.

Trent carefully measured his words as he raised his head to establish eye contact with Jake. His voice was calm, steady. "I know you have questions. I'm sure everyone does. I can't really answer them right now, but I can tell you that very soon all the questions will be answered. There's nothing sinister here. I'm not wanted by the law or being chased by mobsters. All I ask is that you indulge me for a little while longer." His expression became soft, caring, loving. "Cassie is very important to me. The last thing I want is for her to be hurt."

Jake slowly nodded his head in agreement. "All right. Everyone's taken you at your word for everything so far. I guess a little while longer won't hurt. But for Cassie's sake I hope you're being straight with me."

The distinguished man in his fifties stepped off the ferry and headed straight for the motel. He had called ahead to set up an appointment with Bob Hampton, stating the purpose of the meeting. Harold Brundage had met with Randall Davies and Trent in Randall's office in Seattle, and Trent had prepared the real estate broker for the type of person Bob Hampton was. Harold was ready for the brash, arrogant young man.

"Mr. Hampton, I'll get right to the business at hand. I have a client who is interested in the purchase of this property. The price you are asking is, of course, absurd.''

Bob immediately jumped to his feet. ''Hey—''

''I've taken the liberty of familiarizing myself with the contents of the lease agreement between your late mother and—'' he opened a file folder and glanced at a document, ''—Cassandra Brockton, owner and operator of the restaurant and bar located next door. The lease has been inspected by an attorney versed in the ramifications of real estate law. The terms of the agreement clearly state that upon your mother's death Ms. Brockton has one year in which to exercise an option to purchase, at fair market value, the property on which her business resides.''

Bob sat back down. Like Cassie, he had never really looked over the lease agreement to familiarize himself with all the conditions. The situation had caught him so by surprise that it did not occur to him to ask how Harold Brundage had obtained a copy of the lease.

''Now, Mr. Hampton, your asking price is certainly far and away above fair market value, attested to by the appraisal commissioned by my client. I have a contract here that offers you a fair price. You surely must know that without the income from the lease and the actual real estate the restaurant occupies, what would be left to you is some land with value and a motel of virtually no market value as it now functions.''

Bob tried to recover his composure. ''Oh, yeah? Well, all I have to do is wait out the few remaining months, and the year will be up and she'll have to pay what I ask if she wants to buy the land.''

Harold smiled solicitously. ''Mr. Hampton, I think it would be very foolish of you to assume that Ms. Brockton will remain ignorant of the full implications of her lease agreement with you if you should turn down my client's offer. In fact, I wouldn't be a bit surprised if my client then decided to enter into a business arrangement that would provide her with the means to exercise that option."

Bob sat in stony silence. He was smart enough to know that if he was forced to sell the land to Cassie for the appraised value, he would never be able to get rid of the motel by itself. He also knew he could challenge the conditions in court, but that would leave everything tied up for possibly years. Not wanting to give in too easily, he made one last attempt at maintaining control of the situation. "You tell your client that I'll think it over."

"That will be fine, Mr. Hampton. But don't take too long. My client is also looking at other properties. You will note that this offer is only valid for one week. Here's my card. I'll leave the contract with you. Call me when you've reached a decision." With that, Harold Brundage rose from his chair, shook hands with Bob and left. Bob watched as Harold walked next door to the restaurant, then he looked at the contract. The buyer was something called T.A.N. Inc., a Washington corporation headquartered in Seattle. He shook his head as he wondered what type of a company it was and what they intended to do with the property.

Harold entered the restaurant. He sat at the counter and ordered a cup of coffee. "Are you Cassandra Brockton?" He saw surprise cross her face.

"Yes, I am. Is there something I can do for you?"

"No, not really." He handed her one of his business cards, as Trent had instructed him to do. "I was just next door conducting some business with your landlord. I have a client who has made an offer on the property. I thought you might be interested in knowing."

Cassie looked at the card. "Who's your client?"

"I'm not at liberty to say. I can only reveal that if Mr. Hampton accepts my client's offer it will be a cash deal with immediate possession. At that time your lease agreement will transfer to the new owner. I expect to hear from Mr. Hampton in a few days. I'll be in touch with you at that time."

She watched as Harold Brundage left and boarded the ferry for the mainland. She looked at his card as she shook her head in disbelief.

As soon as she closed the restaurant she went looking for Trent, locating him jogging along the waterfront. "Look at this, Trent." She handed him Harold's card. "This guy has a client who has offered to buy out Bob Hampton. Things could be changing real fast. He wouldn't say who his client is, but it must be some big company because he said the deal would be cash." She looked up at him, capturing the clear blue intensity of his eyes. "I . . . I wonder what's going to happen now?"

"I wouldn't worry about it if I were you." He gave her an encouraging smile as he handed the card back to her. "I'm sure everything is going to be okay. If nothing else, you'll be rid of Bob Hampton."

She frowned as she stared at the card. "He said he should have an answer in a couple of days."

Things were moving along just as he had hoped, just as he had planned. Very soon now things would be perfect. He ran his fingertips softly across her cheek. "Let's go on another picnic. The weather is warm, the sun is shining, the sky is blue and all's right with the world."

"You seem to be in a very good mood. In fact, you've been in an exceptionally good mood ever since you returned from the mainland." She saw the smoldering blue intensity fill his eyes, a look she had grown to know intimately.

"The prospect of spending several hours in a secluded clearing in the woods with a beautiful and very desirable woman would be enough to put the most hardened sourpuss in a good mood. Don't you think so?"

"Mmm. I like the way you think—" she gave him a sly look that radiated pure sex and seduction "—among other things."

He returned her look. "I like the way you do absolutely everything."

It was still daylight when Cassie and Trent returned to her house after their picnic. As he set the picnic basket by the front door she glanced down the hill toward the bar. "I think I'd better check on Mike, make sure he's not swamped." She squeezed his hand. "I'll be right back."

Trent watched as she walked down the path, then he entered the house through his bedroom. His insides stirred with excitement. Things were so close to being settled, so close to being put right. The entire future stretched in front of him, a bright new future that he had not even imagined could be when he had arrived on the island.

He opened his door into the house when he heard her enter through the front door. "How's Mike doing? Everything under control?"

"Yes. Mike said he had a happy-hour rush but things have since settled down to a manageable roar." She slipped her arms around his waist as he enclosed her in his embrace.

A slightly troubled look crossed her face. As much as she would rather have been swept up in the whirling vortex of sensuality that emanated from Trent, she was not able to clear her mind of other things. "I wonder what's going to happen, if someone's actually going to buy out Bob Hampton. I never really gave it any serious thought before now."

"Don't worry so much." He twined his fingers in her hair then held her head against his shoulder as he tried to alleviate her fears. "I'm sure everything will work out just fine."

A sigh of resignation escaped her lips. "I hope so. What's that old saying…better the devil you know than the one you don't? What if this new owner moves in and changes everything? What if it's some big company that decides to remodel the motel and add a restaurant? I'm worried, Trent. I can't help it."

He tightened his embrace. Just a little more time, just a while longer and everything would be out in the open and done. He placed a tender kiss on her forehead then scooped her up in his arms and carried her up the stairs.

He placed her gently on the edge of the bed, wrapped her in his arms and held her against his body. Nothing more—he just held her, reveling in her closeness. He felt the slight tension in her body, tension caused by her concern over the changes in the wind. He stroked her hair and kissed her forehead. She was so special, so important to his life. "Your muscles are tense and knotted. Try to relax. I promise you everything is going to work out just fine."

She raised her head and looked at him, her troubled hazel eyes questioning and searching. "How can you promise me that? You don't know what's going to happen any more than I do."

His insides were torn apart. He wanted to ease her worries, but there were still too many loose ends. "I'll make everything okay. I won't let anything bad happen to you, I promise.''

She snuggled into his embrace. ''Whenever I'm with you I really do believe that nothing bad can happen, that everything really will be all right.'' She sighed audibly as a shudder moved through her body. She tentatively continued with the other situation that had her worried—far more worried than Bob Hampton selling the property. ''What are your plans for the future, Trent? Do you go away as mysteriously as you arrived? I know I have no right to pry into your personal business and I've tried very hard not to, but I have to know. Is that why you went to the mainland, to make some kind of arrangements for the future?''

He looked into the depth of her eyes, saw her fears and felt her anxiety. He had to tell her something. He cupped her face in his hands, lowered his head and covered her mouth with his—no heated passion, just a soft, loving kiss. ''I did go to the mainland to make arrangements for the future, to take care of some business matters.'' He felt the shudder move through her body. ''But I'm not leaving. I made arrangements to stay. If you want me out of your life, you're going to have to tell me to go away.''

He saw the tears well up in her eyes, saw the combination of relief and joy that covered her face. He hugged her tightly against his body, rocking her in his embrace.

Her voice quavered. ''Promise me something.''

''What's that?''

''Promise me you'll never lie to me. Nothing could ever be so bad that it can't be worked out if we're just honest with each other.''

A cold shudder swept through him. Technically he had never actually lied to her—but it was a mighty thin line. ''You're very important to me. I promise I'll do everything I can to make you happy." It was not the promise she had asked for, but it would have to do for right now.

"I've never been so happy in my entire life." Tears of joy trickled down her cheeks. Her overwhelming love filled her being. It had not happened the way she thought it would. She had pictured this scene several times in her mind, and it had always been similar to what had happened when he had bought her the painting—the overwhelming joy and elation bubbling over from within, the unbridled excitement. The actuality, however, was much quieter. It had been soft and warm, the kind of feeling that lasted a lifetime. The reality that she failed to recognize was that he had not said he loved her. She had simply assumed it to be so. Before she could say anything else, he captured her mouth with his.

They each discarded their own clothes in a heap on the floor, a rapidly escalating passion controlling their movements. He laid her back against the pillows as he smothered the silkiness of her skin with his burning kisses.

Her hands feverishly stroked and caressed his hot skin as her bare legs tangled with his. They were both gripped in the deepest throes of passion, oblivious to everything except their searing desire for each other.

He cupped her firm breast in the warmth of his hand then teased her nipple with his tongue. He suckled at one breast, then the other, the heat of his passionate desires igniting a fire in her that threatened to consume her in an incendiary inferno.

Cassie was lost in a swirling cloud of ethereal rhapsody. Her tactile senses were aflame with reckless abandon. She wanted more, she could not get enough of him. She had to touch him, taste him—all of him. Her feverish lips danced ravenously over his chest. Her fingers left fiery trails across his tingling skin as her mouth moved closer and closer to the rigid intensity that rose between his trembling thighs.

She lowered her head and provocatively tasted his hardness. Trent's head jerked back into the pillow as a growl of intense pleasure, born deep within him, climbed out of his throat and escaped his lips.

He again consumed her mouth while caressing the length of her body. He tickled his fingers across the soft skin of her inner thigh. When he reached her moist heat, he felt her body shudder and heard her quick intake of breath. His own arousal reached out toward her. He took her hips firmly in his hands and lifted her onto him, filling her velvet-soft interior as she tightly encased his masculine desire.

With her knees straddling his torso, she closed her eyes in all-consuming passion as her labored breathing became even more ragged. She instinctively rocked back and forth in a slow, undulating manner as they both relinquished their control to the deliciously sweet sensations that rapidly built within them.

He made a low throaty sound as she ran her fingers through his thick blond hair then brought her mouth to his, her being aflame with desire. He wrapped his arms around her, holding on to her tightly as if he were afraid she would disappear should he let go. He slowly rolled her over on her back as they remained united in a burning oneness, their hips moving in harmonious union.

Trent's kisses were sweet, tender and loving while at the same time conveying the depth of the torrid passion that surged through his being. The climax of his physical sensations shuddered through his body as the rapture claimed him. He buried his face in her hair in an effort to muffle any words that might have accidentally escaped, wanting to tell her of his deep feelings, but unable to.

She had never before experienced the delights attainable at the far-flung boundaries their lovemaking reached that night. Every place he touched her, everything he did—all of it provided a sensual ecstasy she had never before known. He was the center of her existence, the core of her universe around which everything revolved.

They lay quietly in each other's arms, savoring the delicious aura that enveloped them. Her head rested against his damp chest, and his strong heartbeat filled her with a sense of well-being. "I'm so happy, Trent. I never believed it was possible to be this happy." She raised her head and brushed her lips against his.

She thought briefly about the future, speculating on what she hoped would be, how their lives together could be arranged. He had told her everything would be all right, but she still had worries about the sale of the motel and the land. She snuggled closer to the warmth of his body and drifted into a contented sleep. She loved him, that was all that mattered. Everything else could be worked out.

Trent kissed her tenderly on the cheek. The intensity of his love for her was no longer something he could deny or shove aside. Just a little more time, that was all he needed.

Nine

The next few days were filled with an expectant undercurrent of excitement, like a low-level voltage surge that tingles but does not hurt. Trent was more anxious than Cassie to hear about Bob Hampton's decision. Logically, the only smart thing for Bob to do would be to accept the offer. But if there was one thing that he had noticed about Bob it was that the arrogant young man was not particularly smart.

Cassie radiated her happiness—it showed in her every word and every gesture. She seemed to be floating in air, or rather on a cloud of euphoria. Anne and Charlene had both commented on it, and Mike had grudgingly admitted that she seemed happier than usual. Only Jake seemed to be a little reticent in his attitude, a situation that went unnoticed by Cassie.

"Cassie, honey, you've certainly been in a good mood lately." Jake carefully formulated his words. "Is there something I don't know about that's causing it? Anything you'd like to talk about?''

"Jake, I'm in such a good mood that even Bob Hampton—'' she glanced out the front window ''—who's hurrying up the walk as we speak, can't dampen my spirit. Things have never been so perfect."

Jake swiveled around on the counter stool and watched as Bob entered the restaurant. As usual, the young man swaggered arrogantly up to the counter. "I just thought I'd let you know I've sold everything. I just signed the contracts and sent them back to the real estate broker. We talked on the phone. He'll have a cashier's check for me and I'll be packed and out of here by the end of the week."

A look of wariness came into Cassie's eyes. "Who's the new owner? When will they be here?"

"I guess it won't hurt anything if I tell you. The new owner is some Seattle company, T.A.N. Inc. I haven't any idea who they are or what they do. The broker, Harold Brundage, is handling everything for them. I imagine he'll be in touch with you." Bob looked around, as if for the last time. "Well, don't think it hasn't been fun. See ya!" With that, Bob turned and left the restaurant.

Cassie looked at Jake. "I wonder what happens now." A worried look quickly darted across her face. "If some big corporation is buying the place, that could mean lots of changes. That's been my biggest worry, that some company would buy up everything then remodel the motel and add a restaurant. That would put me out of business."

"Don't you think it's time you had that lease of yours carefully analyzed? Maybe there's some clause about no competing business being allowed on the property. Bessie Hampton was a fair and honest woman. She and Sofie were the closest of friends. I'm sure there must be something in the lease that protected Sofie."

"Well, maybe Trent could look at it for me. He seems to have a real good grasp of things like this."

Jake shook his head. "I'd feel better if you had an attorney look at it. Sometimes legal wording can be very confusing and deceptive."

An involuntary laugh escaped her throat, a laugh indicating her disdain. She did not see Trent enter the restaurant and come up behind her. "Legal wording being deceptive? Anything and everything about an attorney is deceptive. They can look you right in the eye and say something that sounds like one thing but actually means something entirely different."

A quick shudder darted up Trent spine at the sound of her words. He had planned to tell her that night—tell her about everything. He had talked to Randall Davies, knew that Bob Hampton had accepted the offer. The architectural plans for the remodeling had already been drawn up and he had the construction company standing by to start work. The remodeling would begin as soon as Bob vacated the property.

"Cassie..." His voice was tentative.

"Trent!" She whirled to face him, surprised to hear his voice coming from directly behind her. "Guess what! Bob Hampton was just here. He accepted the offer for the property. It was from some company in Seattle. I never heard of them before—T.A.N. Inc. Have you ever heard of them?" Her face reflected her caution and wariness, her uncertainty about what was going to happen.

"I would imagine that as soon as all the papers are filed they'll be getting in touch with you." He offered her a confident smile as he lightly tickled his fingertips across her cheek. "Stop worrying. Everything will be fine."

She furrowed her brow in concentration. "I sure hope you're right."

Trent glanced at the clock. "I've got some things to do. We'll talk about this tonight." He gave her hand a warm squeeze and flashed a teasing smile. "Stop frowning like that. It makes you look like you're worried about something."

Just the feel of his skin against hers, the warmth of his touch, made all her fears and worries vanish. Nothing bad could happen as long as he was there. She returned his smile and squeezed his hand. "Okay, we'll talk about it tonight." Her gaze followed him as he strolled out the door and down the front walk.

She did not notice the look of concern on Jake's face as he rose from the stool, his gaze also following Trent's movements. Trent had asked his indulgence for a little while longer. He had agreed, but he was feeling very uneasy about it. There were too many new and strange things happening. Jake did not like a lot of change. He studied the expression on Cassie's face. It was so clear how much she cared for Trent. He again hoped that Trent was being honest with him, that Cassie would not be hurt.

The rest of Cassie's shift passed quickly. Upon closing the restaurant, she went to her office to take care of the bookkeeping chores. When she finished with the restaurant business she turned her attention to the box that had been delivered to her that day. Her excitement mounted as she opened the package and removed the contents.

She pulled out the old newspapers that had been used as packing material then removed the plaques from the carton, propped them up against the wall and studied them. They were exactly what she had hoped they would be—she liked them very much. She gathered them up and carried them downstairs. She would ask Trent to hang them in the bar as soon as he got back. Her brow wrinkled slightly, as she wondered where he had rushed off to in such a hurry.

"Hi." Trent's greeting was casual but warm. Things were moving so fast now. He had spent the afternoon on the phone with his office in Beverly Hills, followed by a series of calls setting a whole new pattern of events into motion.

"Hi, yourself." She proudly displayed her new acquisitions. "I ordered these for the bar—they just arrived. What do you think of them?"

He picked up one plaque then the other and studied them. "I like them." He flashed her a warm smile as he set them on the table. "Do you want me to hang them on the wall for you? Which wall do you want them on?"

"I think that empty space by the front door. What do you think? Will they look good there?"

"Well…" He gave her a teasing grin and a quick wink. "This isn't exactly my line of work. I think we might have to negotiate a payment of some sort in exchange for this service. Wouldn't you say so?"

A look of innocence covered her face. "Really? Whatever did you have in mind?"

He squeezed her hand, then picked up the plaques and started for the front door. "That's something else we can discuss later."

After he left she looked around the living room as a feeling of restlessness settled over her. There was a certain level of anxiety coursing through her system. She wanted to discuss the property sale with Trent. She would show him her lease and get his opinion as soon as he returned from hanging the plaques. She went into her office to get the lease agreement from the files.

The newspaper mess was piled on the floor next to the box the plaques had been shipped in. One by one she smoothed out the crumpled pages then folded them. She would add them to the recycle stack at the corner market.

She picked up the last section of newspaper and smoothed it out, then glanced casually at the contents. *It's the* Los Angeles Times *from last April.* She turned to the second page, then back again. *It appears to be the entertainment section. These pictures look like some kind of movie premiere party.*

A cold chill slowly spread through her body. One of the photographs, a candid picture of two people laughing and drinking champagne, leaped off the page and grabbed her attention. The man in the picture, the man dressed in a tuxedo with the sultry brunette in the low-cut gown hanging on his arm . . . he looked just like Trent. A hard lump formed in her throat and her mouth went dry.

She closed her eyes. She was afraid. She was afraid to read the caption under the picture, afraid of what it might say. Slowly she focused on the photograph, then on the words beneath it. *"Prominent Beverly Hills attorney Trent Nichols with his companion, French actress Monique Deveroux."* Her eyes filled with tears. Her body trembled. There had to be some sort of logical explanation . . . maybe one of those weird coincidences of someone having the same name and bearing a resemblance. . . . After all, it was a newspaper photo and not really all that clear.

Try as she might she could not convince herself that it was some strange quirk of fate. The rapidly sinking feeling inside her body told her the truth. Trent was someone rich and important from Beverly Hills, someone who dated French actresses, someone who moved in the high social set—a shudder passed through her—an attorney, another deceitful, lying attorney. The reality of her accidental discovery enveloped her like a cold, wet fog with long tentacles of ice that reached out to strangle the life from her. She felt numb.

It must have been half an hour before she finally stood and left the office, the newspaper clutched in her hand. She could not make any sense of it. Nothing made sense. Surely there had to be some sort of logical explanation. When Trent returned she would ask him about it. It had to be a mistake of some kind. He would have an explanation, he would clear up the confusion—he would make everything okay.

Trent finished mounting the plaques on the wall. Just as he was about to leave he was drawn into a conversation with a couple of the local residents with whom he had formed a casual friendship over the time he had been there. He tried to get away as soon as he could. He smiled to himself as a warm feeling enveloped him. There were so many important plans for the future that he and Cassie needed to discuss—not the least of which was his finally being able to tell her of his deep love for her. He had so much to tell her, so much to explain to her, and it all had to be done that night.

First thing in the morning he absolutely had to go to Seattle. There were papers to sign, and he had to make arrangements for a cashier's check for Bob Hampton, which would require a transfer of funds from Beverly Hills. The timely delivery of the cashier's check was the pivotal point of the entire transaction. There could be no delay.

An anxious excitement pounded in his chest as he walked up the path to the house. He entered through his bedroom, then quickly climbed the stairs to the second floor. A slight frown wrinkled his forehead. He did not see Cassie, and her bedroom light was turned off. "Cassie . . . Cassie, where are you?"

"I'm right here."

He whirled at the sound of her voice, a sound that sent a slight tremor of trepidation up his spine. Her voice was flat, almost cold—devoid of any and all emotion. She stepped out of her darkened bedroom and into the light of the hall. Her face was drawn, her expression blank and her eyes . . . he had never seen so much pain in anyone's eyes before. His insides twisted into a thousand knots. Something was horribly wrong.

He immediately stepped to her, folded her in his embrace and pulled her body against his. His voice carried all the anxiety that crashed through him. "What's wrong, Cassie? Are you all right?"

She pushed away from him. Her mouth went dry and her throat felt tight. She had difficulty swallowing. "It's this, Trent." Her hand trembled as she handed him the newspaper. "Can you explain this?" A flicker of hope tried to pierce the despair she felt. "It's some kind of mistake, isn't it? Please, tell me it's not true."

He saw the tears well up in her eyes and heard the halting catch in her voice. An overwhelming feeling of impending disaster engulfed him. He took the paper from her hand and looked at it. A hard jolt pounded inside his chest. He immediately recognized the photograph.

His head snapped up, his eyes wide with shock. She saw the panic cross his face. The look said it all. There was no mistake. The tiny glimmer of hope she nurtured deep inside her being flickered then faded into darkness, only to be replaced by a horrible pain. Her voice was a mere whisper as she bowed her head and stared blankly at the floor. "I see."

The smooth, controlled manner of the experienced trial attorney disappeared. The dispassionate, analytical demeanor that usually got him what he wanted failed to materialize. He stood in stunned silence as his world began to crumble around him. He finally forced out some words. "Cassie, it's not what you think. I was going to tell you tonight—tell you everything about me, clear up all the misunderstandings." The panic in his voice clearly defined his tenuous position.

"You promised me you would never lie to me, but you did." The pain was almost more than she could bear. "You lied to me about *everything.*"

He grabbed her shoulders, tried to pull her toward him. Before he could wrap his arms around her she shoved away from him. He took a calming breath. "I didn't lie to you. I've never lied to you."

She riveted her stare on him, her hurt giving way to anger. "Never lied to me?" Her voice became louder. "*Never lied to me?* Everything you've ever said to me has turned out to be a lie."

He grabbed her shoulders again. She verged on hysterics, sobs wracking her body as tears streamed down her cheeks. "Listen to me." He shook her, gently but firmly. "Cassie, listen to me. I never said anything about who I was. I never even said I had arrived on the ferry. That was your assumption."

She glared at him as she tried to twist free of his grasp. "The spirit of the law, counselor—not just the letter of the law. To knowingly allow an erroneous assumption to stand as truth is the same thing as a lie. You deceived me.'' She broke free and darted for her bedroom. Her final words were barely audible. ''You deceived me about everything.'' She slammed the door before he could reach her. The lock clicked from the inside.

Trent tried the door. She had locked it before he could stop her. ''Open this door, Cassie.'' He rattled the door handle. His voice grew louder, his frustration clearly defined. ''Open this door right now!'' He waited a moment, hoping for some response. He heard nothing. He doubled up his fists and pounded on the door. ''Are you going to open this door or am I going to break it down?''

Finally she spoke, her voice soft and full of pain. ''Go away. I don't want to ever see you again.''

He put all his force behind his shoulder and shoved into the door, then a second time and a third. Finally he felt the door give. One more hard shove and it broke open. ''I'm going to make you listen to me.''

''Get out of here!'' She screamed at him, her anger at full tilt. *''Get out of my house!''* He stood his ground, making no effort to leave. She seized the first thing within her reach, a book, and hurled it at him.

Trent's quick reflexes kept the book from striking its mark. Before she could recover from her failed attack he grabbed her wrist and pulled her hard against his body. He held her tightly in his embrace, his arms pinning her arms to her sides while he twined his fingers in her hair and held her head so she could not break away. His mouth came down hard on hers, devouring her with a combination of anger and passion.

She struggled in his arms, desperately wanting to break free of the unwelcome desires he stirred in her. She could not breathe. His heated passion seemed to have sucked all the oxygen from the room.

He relaxed his tight hold on her a little bit, but did not release her from the heated passion of his kiss. She gradually went limp in his arms—not fighting, not responding, not even reacting. He could deal with her fight and her anger, but not with her indifference. He finally released her.

Her voice held no emotion of any kind. "Now, if you're through with whatever it is you're trying to prove, you can take your lies and your deceit and leave my house—" a sob caught in her throat "—and leave my life."

He grabbed her shoulders, his voice filled with the deep emotion surging through him. "Don't do this to me, Cassie. Don't shut me out. We can work this out. Don't close your life off from me. Please don't."

"Shut you out?" Her face twisted in anguish and her words were forced. "I willingly opened my home to you, my life to you, my heart to you...." Her words broke off as she tried to control a sob. "And in return you lied to me and deceived me. You once told me if I wanted you out of my life I'd have to ask you to go...well, I'm asking you to go—now."

Trent closed his eyes for a moment as he tried to compose his rising panic. He leaned his face toward hers, but she turned her face away. He took a calming breath as he studied her for a long moment, then spoke softly as he tried to bring calm and rationale to the situation. "It's true that I'm an attorney with a law practice in Beverly Hills. I'm also a man who, over the past year, has grown more and more dissatisfied with his life. I arranged to take a three-month sabbatical from my practice and use that time to think out my future. I took my boat—"

"Your boat!" She glared at him through her tear-filled eyes. Then suddenly everything drained from her and she had no energy left. Her voice was a mere whisper. "Of course! The mysterious yacht from California. The final piece of the puzzle." Her body trembled as she tried to control her sobs.

Trent took another calming breath and continued. "I took my boat and headed up the coast with no particular plan or destination in mind. A friend of mine, an attorney in Seattle, asked me to do him a favor. That's the reason I came to the island, why I was here when you, literally, fell into my life."

He saw the look in her eyes, a distant look that told him she was not really listening to him, probably not even hearing his words. "Cassie..." It was as if she was not even there. He tried again. "You were a breath of spring, breathing new life into my winter. I almost corrected your assumption at the very beginning, but the anger and bitterness in your voice when you mentioned that your ex-husband was an attorney stopped me. I thought it was only a harmless little deception. It didn't occur to me at that time that you would very soon be the most important thing in my life. I never thought the deception would get so out of hand. The last thing in the world I wanted to do was hurt you." He tried again to enfold her in his embrace.

She stood there like a cold statue, not reacting to his words or his touch. She tried her best to shut out the sound of his voice. She felt empty inside. She wished she felt numb. That way she would not be able to feel the pain.

He placed his fingertips under her chin and lifted her face so that he could see into her eyes. She closed her eyes, refusing to look at him. "I love you, Cassie. I love you with all my heart and soul." He felt the shudder move through her body. "I'm sorry that I've hurt you. I can't do anything to change the past, but I can promise you that I'll do everything I can to make it up to you. I can promise you one other thing, too. I can promise you my undying love until the end of time."

Cassie finally managed to find her voice, to force out some words. How she had longed to hear him say those very words but now it was too late, it was too late for everything. Her voice was hollow, reflecting the emptiness she felt inside. Her words were barely audible. "Don't, Trent. Don't say anything else. You've totally betrayed my trust and my love. Leave my house and leave my life." She turned away from him, tears streaming down her cheeks. She felt a gaping wound where her heart used to be. Never in her entire life had she felt as alone as she did at that very moment.

His words were soft, his voice containing all the pain he felt—nothing was hidden. "I'll sleep on my boat tonight." He added a hopeful glimmer to his words. "We'll talk some more in the morning."

"There's nothing more to talk about. I could never love someone who lied to me. Make sure you take all your belongings with you. Anything you leave will be thrown away. Take your boat and go. I never want to see you again."

He made one more attempt to hold her, reaching his arms out to her, but she stepped out of the way. His voice pleaded with her, his pain and anguish clearly conveyed through his every word. "Please, Cassie, don't throw away our future like this." He took a calming breath, then continued. "I have very pressing business in Seattle tomorrow, business that can't wait. But as soon as I get back—"

She turned away from him. "We have no future. Don't bother coming back. You're not welcome here." She could not say any more. Convulsive sobs took over her body. She felt him place his hand on her shoulder, but she immediately jerked away from his touch.

Trent stood quietly for a moment, trying to pull his thoughts together. "Cassie—"

"Go away."

An audible sigh of despair escaped his lips. "All right. We'll talk as soon as I get back from Seattle." He paused before turning away. "I love you."

She heard him leave the room and descend the stairs. She closed her bedroom door, then collapsed on top of the bed. Burying her head in her pillow, she sobbed so hard her entire body shook. Her life was over. She would never be able to love anyone as much as she loved Trent.

Trent sat on the edge of the bed, not quite sure what to do. If only he had told her yesterday, before she found out on her own. If only...he shook his head slowly from side to side. All the if onlys in the world could not change what had happened. He closed his eyes and took a calming breath. He loved her so very much. Without a shred of enthusiasm he mechanically went about the job of gathering his belongings. He would be leaving first thing in the morning.

Trent made a final check of the room. Everything was exactly as he had found it—with one exception. On the nightstand next to the bed rested an envelope.

He paused at the outside door, turned and gave one last look at the room. Some of the happiest moments of his life had been spent in that house. But his business in Seattle could not wait. Maybe a day or two apart would give Cassie some breathing space, give her some time to collect her emotions. He turned and walked outside, hoping and praying that he was not making another mistake. He walked listlessly toward the harbor, his heart heavy with his sorrow.

Ten

Cassie spent a terrible night. She tossed and turned but only managed to sleep in short spurts, and fitfully, at that. It was only four o'clock in the morning and she was wide awake. She lay in bed staring at the ceiling. She wanted to stay in bed, stay under the covers where it was safe. She did not ever want to go out again, but she knew she had to, starting with going to work. Reluctantly she forced herself out of bed.

Trent's night was every bit as miserable as Cassie's. He had not been on his boat since his arrival on the island, and he felt confined. He paced up and down the deck, went in and out of every cabin. He tried to sleep, but he could not relax. He may have dozed off sometime during the night, but he was not certain of it.

He found himself in a real quandary, and was not sure exactly how to proceed. He glanced at his watch. It was only four o'clock in the morning. He shook his head and climbed out of bed. It was no use trying to sleep—he was just too upset. He had to try to talk to Cassie again before he left. He would catch her before she went to work. He had to make her listen to reason.

As he walked up the path toward her house he saw the upstairs light on and knew she was awake. If her night had been anything like his, she had not gotten much sleep. He went directly to the bedroom door entrance and tried the handle. To his surprise, the door opened. She had not even come downstairs to lock it. He entered the house and saw that the envelope he had left by the bed was still there. He tried the inside door. It, too, was unlocked. He did not like that—she had been in the house all alone all night with the doors unlocked. He cautiously made his way up the stairs.

Cassie sat on the edge of her bed, unable to move. Her insides were empty and she was drained of all energy and feeling. Her mind snapped to attention when she heard someone coming up the stairs.

"Cassie?" He called to her, then listened intently, waiting for her to answer him.

She heard his voice. Before she could control her true feelings from deep within, the total and complete love she felt for him, she jumped to her feet and rushed for the door. Then she stopped, allowing her hurt and anger to take control. "If you don't get out of my house right now I'm going to call the police. You're trespassing." Her insides shivered as she watched the door swing open.

Her eyes were red and puffy, with dark circles underneath. Her hair was mussed. Her eyes . . . the pain that showed in her eyes was almost more than he could stand. He tried to keep his voice calm. "We're going to talk this out. I have to leave for Seattle but, I don't want to go with things between us like they are. We're going to start with my telling you that I love you more than anything in the world and nothing you say or do is going to change that. Furthermore, I know you love me.''

Her voice was flat. ''You're wrong. I don't love you. You lied to me.''

''You know that's not true, Cassie. You do love me and I never lied to you. The only thing I'm guilty of is holding back some pieces of the complete picture. That was wrong of me.''

''There! You admit you deceived me.''

''Yes, I admit that I was not completely honest with you, but I never meant to hurt you.'' He stepped closer to her, wanting with every fiber of his being to wrap her in his embrace and never let go of her. ''Every time I wanted to tell you I would hesitate, not knowing how to tell you, I was so afraid I'd lose you.'' He reached out for her, drew her into his embrace and pulled her body against his. He felt her muscles stiffen. ''I love you, Cassie. You know that's true. No matter how hurt and angry you are right now, you know I love you.''

She quickly pushed away from the temptation of his touch. His words made sense, but, no, she would not allow it. He had lied to her, deceived her. He had betrayed her love and trust. ''I don't know any such thing. Please, just go away. Leave me alone, leave my island.''

With a swiftness that startled her he shoved her onto the bed, then quickly covered her body with his. His mouth came down hard on hers, the fires of his passion consuming her wholly. Just as swiftly he released her. ''This isn't over, Cassie.''

Her words were barely above a whisper, the heated passion that surged through her more to blame than her hurt and anger. ''Yes, it is, it's completely over. You made a fool out of me. I won't allow you to do it again.''

The intensity of his sky blue eyes burned into her consciousness. His look held her captive, the power of his magnetic aura imprisoned her. "No, it's not over, not by a long shot. It will never be over. I love you too much for that to ever happen." He stood and took a calming breath. "Cassie, this is far from over. You've not seen the last of me." He gave her one final look of longing, then turned and left her bedroom.

Cassie stood on the bluff overlooking the small harbor. The stiff ocean breeze whipped her short tawny hair against her face. She hugged her arms around her shoulders as her small body trembled, possibly from the cold, damp air but more likely from emotional turmoil. Tears brimmed her eyes then trickled down her cheeks, and a sob caught in her throat.

She watched as the sleek powerboat made its way toward open water. She had told him to leave, told him to get out of her life forever. She did not need him—his lies and his deceit. A shudder moved through her body. He had deceived her about everything else—how could she believe he really loved her? Another sob caught in her throat as she turned away. She could not bear to watch any longer.

Slowly she made her way back to the house. Charlene had already opened the restaurant. Cassie needed to get ready for work. That would probably be the best thing for her. Work would take her mind off her overwhelming pain and her all-encompassing sorrow.

Cassie quickly hustled off to take care of a table. There was no mistaking the look of despair that covered her face. Charlene rushed over to Jake, lowering her voice to a very quiet whisper. "Something's wrong. Things aren't too busy here—I can handle it alone. Do something, Jake.'' Her eyes pleaded. "Go to her, find out what's wrong.''

Cassie hurried past Jake on her way to refill coffee cups. He grabbed her arm, bringing her to a halt. Without a word he took the coffeepot from her and handed it to Charlene, then forcefully escorted her out through the back door and up the path toward her house.

"Jake, what's the meaning of this?'' She tried to wiggle her arm free of his grasp, but he held her too tightly. "What do you think you're doing?''

They reached the front porch. "I've lived a lot of years and I've seen lots of people's pain but I've never seen a look like the one covering your face. Now, do you want to sit here on the swing and talk or would you rather go inside?'' His soft brown eyes intently studied her reaction to his words.

"Talk? I don't have time to talk. I need to be at work.'' She averted her gaze, unable to hold his look.

"What you *need*, Cassie, honey, is to tell me what's wrong. Why do you look like you've just lost your best friend in the whole world?'' He loosened his grasp on her arm. "Is that it? Have you lost your best friend?''

"I . . . I really don't know what you're talking about. Now, please, let me go back to work.'' She felt tears well up in her eyes and turned her head away from his gaze, not wanting him to see her face.

"We'll go inside.'' Jake opened the door and escorted her inside the house. "It's Trent, isn't it? What's happened? Is he all right? He's not hurt, is he?''

"He's gone. . . .'' Cassie burst into tears and buried her head against Jake's chest. "I sent him away. I told him to leave and never come back.''

This certainly was not what he had expected. He put his arms around her and tried to comfort her as best as he could. "What happened, Cassie, honey? I thought the two of you were getting on real good. It was just so obvious how much you two liked each other."

"You were right, Jake. I should never have trusted him. He deceived me. He's an attorney, Jake, a Beverly Hills attorney—another lying, deceitful attorney." She could not say any more as sobs wracked her body, her tears soaking into his shirt.

"And you love him." Jake's words were soft. "Isn't that right, Cassie, honey?" He felt so bad for her. She was obviously hurting very deeply. He comforted her in his own awkward way. It upset him to see her so unhappy. "That's it, go ahead and cry. Get it out of your system." He did not know what to say to her. He wished he knew what had happened, how all of this had come about. *An attorney from Beverly Hills,* he thought. *Well, that explains a lot.*

He kept his arm around her shoulders as he steered her toward the couch in the living room. She needed to talk about what had happened. She could not leave it bottled up inside her. He sat next to her. "Come on, now, tell me what happened."

Cassie continued to sob uncontrollably, pulling comfort from her friend's caring and concern. Jake did not say anything; he allowed her to cry until she had no more tears to shed. He pulled a clean handkerchief from his pocket and handed it to her. "You stay right here, I'll get you a glass of water." He hurried to the kitchen and returned with the glass. She drank down the entire thing.

"Do you feel better, Cassie, honey? Can you talk about it now?" He took the empty water glass from her.

She took several gulping breaths as she tried to calm herself. Finally, in a voice quaking with the strong emotions that still surged through her, she began to talk. She told Jake what had happened the night before—told him about finding the newspaper article, about confronting Trent with the photo, asking for some explanation, hoping against hope that it was all some huge misunderstanding.

"What did he say?"

"He didn't say anything."

"Come now, Cassie. Do you mean that you told him to leave and he turned around and walked out without saying anything? That doesn't make any sense. He must have said something to you before leaving."

She tried to speak between sobs. "He told me he hadn't meant to deceive me...told me he had planned to tell me everything last night...told me..." Tears trickled down her cheeks. "He told me...told me he loved me." The sobs cut off whatever words she had left.

Jake's mind worked in a very orderly and analytical manner. Why would a successful attorney wander into the restaurant and suddenly decide, on the spur of the moment, to stay on the island for an apparently indefinite amount of time? It would seem that he would need to return to his law practice. And if Trent had said he intended to tell her everything, then perhaps he had decided not to leave. If that was the case, then it could only be because he loved her. There must be more, something else that he had said. He was jarred from his thoughts by Cassie wiggling out of his arms. She wiped the tears from her cheeks as she headed toward the bathroom.

Jake took advantage of Cassie's momentary absence to check the guest room. He wanted to see if Trent had left anything behind, perhaps some personal belongings that would allow the door of communication between the two of them to be opened again. He would have to contact Cassie to tell her where to send his things or, better yet, he would have to come back to get them.

He looked in the closet, then opened each and every drawer, but found everything empty. His disappointment weighed heavily. Then he saw the envelope on the nightstand. He picked it up and carried it into the living room, arriving just as Cassie came out of the bathroom.

He handed her the envelope. Her brow wrinkled as a frown crossed her face. She looked perplexed as she took it from him. "What's this?"

"I don't know. It's addressed to you. I found it on the nightstand next to the bed in the guest room."

She stared at it, almost afraid to look inside. Her eyes filled with tears again as she dumped the contents of the envelope on the table.

Cassie's eyes opened wide as she saw the money—bills and coins scattered across the table, mingled in with a couple of pieces of paper—then she sifted through the array, separating the money from the paper. She turned toward Jake, her expression showing her confusion.

"What have you got there, Cassie?"

"I...I don't know. It's money and—" she picked up one of the pieces of paper "—and the check I gave Trent for working when Mike was sick." She picked up the other piece of paper, a note addressed to her. She sat down and read the note.

My darling Cassie. I love you very much. Whether you admit it or not, you know it's true. I have pressing business in Seattle that affects our future together. Otherwise, nothing you could have said would have made me leave with things so unsettled

between us. The enclosed money is the tips from
when I worked that bar shift. It's rightfully Mike's.
I'll see you in a few days when I've finalized my
business dealings. I love you more than anything,
Cassie. You're my life. Trent.

She stared blankly at the money, not knowing what to
think anymore. She handed Jake the note.

He quickly scanned the words, then handed it back to
her. "This note sounds very sincere to me. What do you
plan to do?"

"Nothing." Anguish covered her face and filled her
voice. "It's all over. He's gone and I'm glad."

"You know you don't mean that. Did you get any sleep
at all last night? You look terrible. You have dark circles
under your eyes."

She tried her best to muster a smile. "You old smooth
talker, that's just the kind of thing a girl wants to hear."

"Why don't you take a nap? Maybe things will be a
little more clear after you've had some sleep. We'll talk
later, okay?" He offered her an encouraging smile.

Concern flooded her face. "I can't do that. I have to
be at work. Charlene is there alone."

"She said she could handle things. If it gets too busy
she can call you. Now, you go upstairs and get some
sleep."

Cassie's confusion was clearly discernible. Her eyes
filled with tears, and she shook her head back and forth.
"I don't know what to do, I don't know what to think."

He put his arm comfortingly around her shoulders and
steered her toward the stairs. "You get some sleep. I'll
check on you later."

When they reached the foot of the stairs she stopped
and turned toward Jake, her eyes questioning. "You

won't tell anyone about this, will you? No one needs to know how far things went. If they insist on some sort of an answer, just tell them . . ." Her gaze dropped to the floor, her shoulders sagging under her despair. "It doesn't matter." Cassie turned and slowly climbed the stairs.

Jake watched her, his heart heavy with his concern over the pain she felt. An attorney. If Trent had been anything but an attorney this entire situation would not have gotten so far out of hand. If only he could have been a stockbroker or a doctor or a banker, anything but an attorney.

Cassie sat on the edge of her bed, her gaze riveted to the painting on the wall—the painting Trent had bought her. Her eyes grew heavy. She lay back and was soon asleep.

Trent did not like leaving with things so unsettled, but he had business to take care of—he had the final papers to sign for the motel purchase, he had to transfer funds for a cashier's check for Bob Hampton, he needed to make a last check on the architect's plans and go over details with the construction people.

He also had Beverly Hills business to settle, things that he needed to tend to in person. He needed to close his house and put it up for sale, pack up his personal belongings and arrange to have them shipped to the island, and take care of the final paperwork so that his law partner could buy him out as they had agreed.

He had discussed having his secretary continue to work for him on the island. She was a widow in her mid-fifties with no particular ties to Southern California, and she had been very receptive to the idea. He wanted a clean break, wanted to sever his Los Angeles business ties and start fresh. He had three weeks' worth of work to do and he was determined to get it done in one week. He did not want to be away from Cassie for longer than a week—especially with things in the precarious state that currently existed.

After leaving the island he docked at Seattle and contacted Randall Davies. The two men finalized the paperwork on Bob Hampton's property and Trent arranged for the cashier's check. Next they double-checked the remodeling plans and Trent gave his instructions to the construction company, making it clear that they would be answering to Randall Davies until Trent returned to the island.

Having taken care of his necessary Seattle business, he caught the next flight to Los Angeles. He would pick up his boat later, when he returned.

He leaned back in his first-class seat and closed his eyes. Images of Cassie, one after the other, flooded his mind's eye—the way her nose crinkled when she laughed, the sparkle of her hazel eyes when she was excited and the fire when she was angry, the creamy-smooth texture of her skin, the honesty that covered her when they shared the intimacies of their love. Their love… everything had to work out. He was staking his entire future and everything he owned on that love.

He nervously went over his mental list of things to do. He had not phoned Cassie since leaving the island. Several times over the past three days he had picked up a phone to do just that, but he had hesitated then replaced the receiver in the cradle. He desperately wanted to talk to her, to hear the sound of her voice, but he did not want to upset her any more than she already was. He wanted to give her time. He wanted to do the right thing, but he just was not sure what the right thing was. He hoped he was not making things worse than they already were.

It was not just Cassie, either. He owed explanations to Jake, Mike and the others—everyone who had accepted him at face value.

One day led into another. They all seemed the same to Cassie. She mechanically progressed through her daily functions—she worked, she ate, she slept. It seemed that work was her only solace. The time that she was busy in the bar or restaurant was time that her pain could be set aside. But her time alone at home, that was the worst of all. She saw Trent's face, heard his voice—he was everywhere.

Now that she had had a few days to reflect, time to get past her hurt and anger, she had to admit that she had been unfair in her accusations. Jake had been right—she had a definite blind spot where attorneys were concerned. Maybe he did have a valid reason for not telling her, for concealing his true identity. She wanted to believe him, wanted it to be so. Why had he not called her, or tried to get in touch with her? She was so confused...and so miserable. Somehow life would go on, but how?

Cassie did not recognize the two men who entered the restaurant.

"Miss Brockton?" The man in the business suit extended his hand toward her. "My name is Randall Davies. I represent the new owner of the property."

A look of wariness covered her face. She had not mentioned it to anyone, other than Trent, but she had been dreading this moment. She did not know what was in store for her now that the sale was final. Trent had told her not to worry, that everything would be all right. Maybe it would have been, but now that he was gone...

"The new owner will be doing some extensive remodeling, starting immediately. This—" he indicated the man with him "—is Steve Alexander. His company will be doing the construction work." Steve and Cassie silently acknowledged the other's presence as Randall continued. "There will be a resident manager for the motel—Grace Edwards. She should be arriving in a few days."

"This new owner." Cassie's voice carried her trepidation. "If he has a resident manager, apparently he doesn't plan to run things himself. Will he be making an appearance? I'd like to meet him."

"He should be here in a few days. He planned to be here today, but business matters delayed him."

"What kind of company is—" she searched her mind for the name Bob had given her "—is T.A.N. Inc.? What do they do?"

"It's primarily a holding company for my client's Washington interests."

"Why would this big corporation be interested in a little motel on this island? What do they plan to do with it? What does the remodeling consist of?"

Trent had warned Randall of Cassie's specific concern. "Don't be alarmed, Miss Brockton. The new owner is fully aware of the business situation as it currently exists. He has no intention of interfering with your livelihood. In fact, I believe his intention is to enter into a business arrangement with you whereby motel guests can avail themselves of your services as part of their stay."

"Who is this person? What's his name?"

"Oh, I'm not at liberty to divulge that information at this time. I can only assure you that you have no cause for alarm in this matter." Randall Davies glanced at his watch, then turned his attention to Steve Alexander. "It's getting late. Let's do a survey." He turned back toward Cassie. "It was nice meeting you, Miss Brockton. I'll be in touch. Goodbye."

She watched as the two men left the restaurant and went next door to the motel. Bob Hampton had moved out two days before, leaving the place locked up. This now made everything official. He was out and the mysterious new owner was in. A resident manager probably meant that the new owner would not be around very much. She wondered what kind of woman this Grace Edwards was and where she came from.

Eleven

Trent vacillated between pleased and impatient. Although he had convinced himself that he could get everything done in a week, he knew, deep inside, that one week was really pushing it too much. But he wanted to get back to the island. As soon as he hit the traffic and congestion of Los Angeles he knew he had made the right decision.

Grace Edwards had been surprisingly pleased with Trent's final suggestion on how things could be handled. He really did not want to lose her. Besides being a first-rate secretary, an efficient office manager and fully qualified to be a paralegal if she chose to take the test, she had a brother who owned three motels and was fully conversant with that type of operation. He had no desire to be confined to the day-to-day running of the motel. Grace would be someone he could trust and, by including the manager's apartment as part of the deal, she would have a free place to live. It was a good arrangement for both of them.

Settling his financial matters—making arrangements to sell his house, transferring bank accounts, having his belongings stored until he knew exactly where to have them shipped, having his cars transported and wrapping up the final loose ends at his Beverly Hills office—was all taking more time than he had originally allotted. He was anxious to get back to Cassie, but knew he had to take care of business first. He did not want to be required to make another trip to Los Angeles to wrap up loose details.

Cassie kept a watchful eye on what the construction people were doing. Judging from the size of the crew, the new owner planned more than just a little cosmetic remodeling. Their activity seemed to be good for her business. In addition to the construction crew eating at the restaurant and stopping in at the bar for a few beers after work, the locals were spending more time indulging their curiosity about what was happening. The large parcel of land allowed for considerable expansion—new construction in addition to the buildings already there.

Each day she watched the harbor for any sign of Trent's return. Each day she jumped every time the phone rang. Each day she felt more and more lost and alone without Trent. Each day her despair increased as she wondered if he would ever come back.

Jake sat with her one day on the porch swing as they drank their early-morning coffee. He pointed toward the motel. "They've sure been working fast. It's amazing how much they've accomplished in such a short time. Have you seen exactly what they're doing over there? They're doubling the size of the motel in square feet but only adding half again as many rooms. Each room is being enlarged and completely upgraded. They're adding a large glass-enclosed hot tub and swimming pool that can be used year-round. The only thing I don't understand is the officelike complex that's being added on the other side of the lobby. It has a separate entrance from the outside in addition to a door off the lobby. It doesn't seem to have any purpose that I can see."

"Someone is sure spending a lot of money. It's a good location. If they make everything really first class without raising the rates too much, they should be very successful." A sigh of resignation escaped Cassie's lips. "I hope Randall Davies was telling me the truth when he said the new owner did not plan to interfere with my business operation. I took that to mean that he would not be adding a restaurant or bar as part of the remodeling."

"I wouldn't worry if I were you, Cassie, honey. I haven't seen anything that looks like that type of expansion. I think it's going to be okay."

She offered him a brave smile. "I'm sure you're right. Now, I've got to go to work." She gave him an affectionate kiss on the cheek. "You're a dear, Jake. I don't know what I'd do without you."

Cassie was just preparing to close the restaurant at two o'clock when an attractive, gray-haired woman in her fifties carrying an attaché case entered through the front door. Her manner was very businesslike as she walked directly toward Cassie. "Miss Brockton?"

"Yes, I'm Cassie Brockton."

The woman smiled and held out her hand. "I'm Grace Edwards, the new manager of the motel. It's a pleasure to meet you."

Cassie tentatively returned her smile and accepted her handshake. "Yes, Randall Davies mentioned your name."

"Things are very rushed at the moment and time is of the essence so, if you don't mind the abruptness, I'd like to get right down to the business at hand."

A wary look crossed Cassie's face as she indicated a booth where they could sit and talk. "Of course, right this way." She locked the door, then joined Grace.

Grace opened her attaché case, withdrew a legal document and handed it to Cassie. "I have here a proposed agreement between the corporation and you that would allow motel guests the convenience of charging food and beverage to their room and paying the entire bill at one time upon checkout."

Before Cassie could say anything, express the doubts and reservations that Grace had been told Cassie harbored, she continued. "As you can see, the corporation would reimburse you for the charges in whatever time increments would be convenient for you—weekly or monthly in lump sums or, if you would prefer, at the time that particular guest checked out. If you'd rather, the corporation would be willing to reimburse you on a daily basis as you incurred the expense rather than having you wait until we were paid. I'll leave this document with you so that you may look it over. If you have any questions, I'll be next door." Grace stood, shook hands with Cassie and left.

Cassie stared at the document in her hands. An incredible feeling of relief settled over her. The new owner was not going to add a restaurant. If she had a contract with the corporation to provide food service, then maybe she could trust that she would be paid. It sounded okay on the surface. She would read the contract later, but did not want to sign it until she met the new owner.

In addition to Grace Edwards, Trent had one more person to move to the island. He needed to take care of Chad Willett. The island would be a perfect place for him.

Chad's mother had been Trent's housekeeper for many years. The boy practically grew up in his house. Mrs. Willett had died the previous year, just two days after Chad's eighteenth birthday. The boy's father had died when Chad was only five years old. It was then that Mrs. Willett had gone to work for Trent.

Chad's teen years had not been easy. He had attended Beverly Hills High School because he and his mother lived at Trent's house. But, unlike the other kids, he did not have a new car and lots of spending money. He had been in and out of various scrapes with the law, nothing too serious but trouble nonetheless.

The one thing Chad seemed to be really interested in was Trent's boat. The boy had taken it upon himself to learn as much about boats as he could. Trent had paid for him to take lessons on how to navigate at sea and how to operate a boat the size of his. He had also seen to it that Chad took a Coast Guard safety class. The boy had not disappointed him—he had eagerly tackled everything.

Since his mother's death Chad had been employed by Trent. His duties included taking care of the boat, cleaning the pool at Trent's house, doing yard work and running personal errands. Trent really did not need a gofer. He was not the type of man who expected people to be at his beck and call. What he did need, however, was to make sure that Chad had a clean place to live, proper food and decent clothes. He had offered to pay for

Chad's further education but the boy had declined the offer, saying he did not want to waste Trent's money—maybe later when he had decided what he really wanted to do.

With Chad, it always came back to the boat. That was his great love. Trent had given it a lot of thought. He explained to Chad what he was doing and asked the boy if he would like to move to the island. He would be employed by Trent's new Washington corporation, and his primary duties would be to take care of the boat and work at the motel. Chad had accepted eagerly. In the back of Trent's mind was the possibility of letting Chad operate the boat as a charter business, another new enterprise of T.A.N. Inc.

All Trent could think of was Cassie—seeing her, hearing her voice, touching her, holding her. He had missed her so much. It had been a very long and busy two weeks, but things were now in place, and it was time to return to the island. He and Chad would be on the first flight from Los Angeles to Seattle in the morning.

One day passed into another for Cassie. It had now been two weeks and she had not heard a word from Trent. There was so much activity going on around her, her days should have been filled and busy—but they were not. The people closest to her tried to cheer her up. Even Mike made a valiant attempt at being upbeat. Everyone knew, without Jake telling them, that the source of her unhappiness was whatever had happened to cause Trent to leave so suddenly.

Cassie had pretty much kept clear of the motel. Her own despair had prevented her from being too curious, but now that things seemed to be nearing completion she took a few minutes to wander next door. She spotted

Steve Alexander and walked over to where he was studying the plans. There were architectural drawings spread across a large worktable. He was studying a section having to do with the glass-enclosed hot tub area.

She picked up a rolled drawing and opened it. She stared blankly for a moment, then her eyes opened wide with shock as she realized what she was seeing. It was an artist's rendering of how the completed project would look. It showed the front of her restaurant remodeled to match the look of the motel and a physical connection between the buildings, an enclosed walkway that appeared to make her restaurant part of the motel.

"What is this?" Her sharp question cut into Steve Alexander's concentration.

Steve wheeled around and immediately recognized the drawing. It had been rolled up in the corner and was part of the overall package of plans from the architect but not part of what they were currently working on. He cautiously weighed his words before answering. "That's just one of the artist's renderings that came as part of the architect's package. It's not part of what we're working on. We don't have any construction plans that go with that drawing."

"But why is it here? Why would the drawing have even been made? My restaurant isn't connected with the motel."

"Gee, I don't know, Miss Brockton. Maybe Grace can answer your question. She's in the lobby."

Cassie rolled the drawing and hurried off. She did not know whether to be angry or upset. She did not like the look of this, the direction it seemed to be taking. She quickly found Grace Edwards. Without saying anything, she unrolled the drawing and spread it out in front of Grace, then looked at her questioningly.

Grace frowned as she stared at the drawing. "That shouldn't be here. It's just a drawing the architect did from photos of the motel. One of the photos also included the restaurant. He didn't understand that even though all the land is owned by the corporation your business is separate." She smiled as she rolled up the drawing. "Please don't let this upset you."

Cassie was not sure exactly what was going on. Some inner sense tugged at her consciousness. Why did it seem that everyone was so concerned about her being upset? Why would these strangers have any knowledge of her history with Bob Hampton or the particulars of her lease arrangement? Maybe Grace considered their conversation over, but she did not. "Who or what is this T.A.N. Inc.? I'd like to meet the new owner before I sign that agreement."

"The owner should be here sometime tomorrow. He's in Seattle right now. I'm sure he'll be in touch with you as soon as he arrives."

Chad docked the boat at the harbor. Trent was very pleased with the way the boy handled everything. As soon as the boat had been secured and hooked up to dockside facilities, Trent sent Chad on to the motel. "Tell Grace I'll see her in a little while. I have a few things to take care of first."

Nervous tension settled in his stomach. The moment was at hand—he would see Cassie and talk to her for the first time in two weeks. He had missed her very much and was uncertain about what her reaction to his return would be. Hopefully the separation had been beneficial, allowing her to sort out her hurt from her love. He took a calming breath to steady his nerves, then changed into a business suit. After making a last-minute check of the papers in his briefcase, he left the boat and headed toward the motel.

Trent looked every bit like the successful, high-powered attorney he was, from the top of his expensively styled thick blond hair to the bottom of his Italian loafers. He went directly to the area where Grace had set up a temporary office.

She looked up from her work and gave him a weary smile. "Well, I see you finally made it."

"How are things coming along?" He looked around at the activity. "Is everything on schedule?"

"Better than on schedule. We're ahead of schedule." She handed him a report, the type of rundown he liked—a quick statement of exactly what had been accomplished, what was left to do and closing comments regarding any related incidents. Trent was able to quickly scan the report and know exactly where things stood.

A frown wrinkled his brow as he got to the bottom of the report. Cassie had come across the drawing showing the motel and restaurant as part of the same complex. He looked up at Grace. "What did she say?"

"She was understandably upset. She's most anxious to meet the new owner, says she won't sign the room-charge agreement until she does."

Grace gave him a look that was a combination of longtime employee who knew how far she could push him and motherly concern. "She's a very nice girl, Trent—and she's very nervous about what's going on here. Don't you think you should be straightening out this mess you've created instead of talking to me?"

It was after two o'clock. The Closed sign had been placed in the window of the restaurant. Trent entered through the bar, immediately spotting Jake and Mike, who were engaged in conversation. He did not like the nervousness and uncertainty that churned in his stomach. He was accustomed to being in charge, to having all the facts at hand. He took a steadying breath.

Mike saw him first. His conversation stopped and he stared. Jake turned to see what had attracted Mike's attention. Trent acknowledged both men in a friendly but businesslike manner. It was Jake who came out of his stunned silence first. He jumped up from the bar stool and ushered Trent into a quiet corner. His voice clearly showed his irritation. "Just where the hell have you been for the past two weeks?"

Trent had not been sure what type of reaction would greet him, but this certainly was not one of the options he had considered. He glanced back at Mike, who was looking at him more with curiosity than with anger. He returned his attention to Jake. "I've been taking care of business, making arrangements so that I could come back here and be able to stay." His voice softened as he glanced toward the restaurant. "How's Cassie doing?"

"Two weeks and not a word from you. How she's doing depends . . . are you here to stay or just passing through? I think she's gotten past the fact that you're—how was it phrased—another lying, deceitful—"

Trent held up his hand and smiled. "I think I get the picture." The smile faded from his face and his manner turned serious. She had obviously told Jake about his true identity. He wondered who else knew. "How much did she tell you, tell everyone?"

"Well, there is no everyone. There's only me and I think she probably told me pretty much all of it. She let me read the note you left."

Trent stared at the floor, his voice soft. "I see." He paused for a moment to collect his thoughts, then looked at Jake. "I owe several people an explanation but, first, I've got to see Cassie. Where is she?"

"She's home, probably in her office."

"I'll see you later, Jake." With that, Trent left the bar and walked up the path toward Cassie's house.

Jake returned to his bar stool and a very perplexed Mike. Mike's words were anxious. "What happened? That guy disappeared wearing a pair of faded jeans and now, two weeks later, he shows up wearing a custom-tailored suit. What did he do, win the lottery or something?"

Cassie sat at her desk finishing up the daily book work from the restaurant. For the past hour her stomach had been doing flip-flops as a nervous tremor darted back and forth through her body, a feeling of foreboding. There were too many things happening. Things were too unsettled. The day was more than half over and there had not been any sign of the new owner of the motel.

She leaned back in her chair and closed her eyes. A vivid image of Trent immediately appeared on the screen of her mind. She had sent him away, insisted he leave, told him to get out of her life. She had been hurt and angry. Now, more than anything, she wished she could take back those words. He had said he would return in a few days, but something had obviously happened to change his mind. Her heart ached as she tried to come to terms with the growing awareness that he really was gone forever.

With a heavy sigh she rose from the chair and went downstairs. She paused at the door of the guest room, then went inside. She stared at the bed and wondered if she would ever be able to stop loving him. The doorbell startled her out of her moment of sorrow.

The afternoon sun glinted off his blond hair. His eyes seemed a much brighter blue than she remembered. He looked very impressive in his charcoal gray suit, and so very handsome. Her heart pounded in her chest as his gaze held her captive. Her throat tightened and her mouth went dry. She was having difficulty believing he was really standing on her porch. She felt tears well up in her eyes, threatening to spill over and trickle down her cheeks. She desperately needed to get her soaring emotions under control. She vacillated between her overwhelming joy at seeing him and her renewed anger at him for not contacting her even once during his two-week absence.

His voice was soft, smooth, sexy and very loving. "They say absence makes the heart grow fonder. Is that true or am I in more trouble than I was before you threw me off your island and told me to never darken your door again?" He hoped a light, almost teasing tact would be a good way to break the initial awkwardness.

She tried to maintain a tough stance. "What are you doing here?"

"May I come in, or do you prefer to discuss our business from opposite sides of a screen door?"

He seemed almost too casual to her. She did not know quite what to make of it. "What business could we possibly have to discuss?"

"Well, for starters, I understand that you refuse to sign the room-charge agreement with the motel until you've met the new owner."

Cassie's eyes widened in surprise as a quick intake of breath passed between her lips. Her tough attitude vanished in a puff of smoke and her insides began to tremble as the full realization of what he had just said sank into her consciousness. Her voice was a mere whisper. "You? You're this T.A.N. Inc.?"

"Trenton Anthony Nichols. I know it's not particularly clever, but I was in a hurry and didn't have time to clear a name search before forming a Washington corporation. So, as you can see, we have lots of business to discuss." The casual manner faded and his face became very serious. "Are you going to let me in, Cassie, or do I need to break down another door?" He had reached his limit—so near to her, yet unable to touch her.

It was difficult for her to assimilate everything that was happening. From out of nowhere he appeared on her porch, not as the mysterious stranger she had fallen in love with but rather as a sophisticated, successful attorney in a custom-tailored suit—an attorney who now owned the land under her business. She did not know what to think, she did not know what to feel. "I haven't repaired the last door you broke."

Trent reached his hand out and touched the screen door with his fingertips. His voice was soft, carrying all the love that coursed through his being. "Please open the door, Cassie. We have lots of things to talk about, much more than just business." He saw the confusion and uncertainty in her hazel eyes as she hesitated. Finally she released the latch on the door, then turned and walked into the living room. He entered the house and closed the door behind him.

Little shivers of excitement shot through her when she felt his hand come to rest on her shoulder. Her pulse raced and her breathing quickened. More than anything she wanted to be wrapped in the embrace of his strong arms. She wanted the pain of the past two weeks to disappear. She tried to calm her breathing.

Trent reached out for her—he had to touch her, feel her warmth. He had never before believed that two weeks could be such a long time. Even though he had been extremely busy, the two weeks had seemed like as many months. He brought her to a halt and turned her to face him. "I'm sorry about your door." The emotions welling up inside him spilled over into his voice. "I'll send someone over to fix it." He pulled her into his embrace, his tenuous composure slipping away. "I love you, Cassie. I love you very much."

As much as she wanted to be strong, to stand her ground against his too-tempting presence, she allowed him to enfold her into his embrace. It felt so good to be back in his arms. The previous two weeks had been pure torture for her. She rested her head against his chest and slowly circled her arms around his waist.

A sob caught in her throat. "How could you keep so many secrets from me if you really loved me? People who love each other are supposed to trust each other and share with each other . . . not hide things from each other. You not only deceived me about who you really were, but now I find that you've deceived me about everything else, too."

He continued to hold her in his embrace. He was not sure how to answer her. "I didn't mean to deceive you. I'm accustomed to making decisions in a hurry and acting on them. It's the way I've always done things. I'll have to learn to handle matters differently now—with your help. I want you to know everything. I don't want there to be any secrets between us."

He felt her tremble. Her words were soft. "I don't know, Trent. I don't know what to think or what to do. You left me a note that said you'd be back in a few days and that was the last I heard. The past two weeks have been miserable. You didn't call, not even once."

He told her laughing that when it was over. "If they asked Cindy, won't cause you in that case you in bed. You bet really say she said proved the body you have all and you can the way I heard. She give was confined in the tangle. Now I am all up in experience.

Twelve

"I know." His voice became almost a whisper. "I didn't know what to say. I didn't want to take a chance of making you even more angry over the phone. I still had too many loose ends to tie together."

He tightened his hold on her, squeezing her so tightly she thought he was going to cut off her breathing. His words were soft, whispered in her ear with more emotion than she thought it was possible for anyone to convey with mere words. "I love you, Cassie. You're my entire life—nothing else matters. Without you I have nothing."

She raised her head and looked into the blue fathoms of his eyes. "I don't even know who you are. I thought I knew, but now I don't."

"Yes, you do. Just because you didn't know what I was doesn't mean you didn't know who I was. I'm the same man who's been here the last several weeks. Maybe the clothes are different and the background isn't what you thought, but the man's the same. You're my life, Cassie. You're the most important thing in the world.''

They stood for a silent moment, then he released her from his embrace. Moving quickly, before she had an opportunity to pull away from him, he cupped her face in his hands and lowered his mouth to hers. All the passion, all the fire, all the gentle caring, all the tenderness, all the love—so many emotions and feelings magically combined into one kiss.

He twined his fingers in her short hair, his mouth devouring hers as he pressed her body tightly against his. He had not intended to grab her like that, but once he had her enfolded in his arms he could not stop himself. She was everything to him. Everything about her excited him.

A swirling cloud of euphoria enveloped her the moment his mouth came in contact with hers. She loved him so much he made her lose all concept of reason and logic. She was so glad he was back. Her last conscious thought was a silent prayer that he was back to stay.

''I've missed you so much.'' His words were breathless in her ear. His lips left fiery trails as his hot kisses smothered her being.

Cassie tried to regain her senses, take control of a situation that was rapidly spiraling beyond what either of them had the ability to contain. ''Please, Trent...'' Her words were husky as she tried to pull away from him. ''Don't do this. I...''

Reluctantly he loosened his grip on her. He twined his fingers in her hair and held her head against his chest. ''I'm sorry, Cassie. I shouldn't have done that. It's just that I love you so much.''

"What's happening?" She looked at him with questioning and wary eyes. "Explain to me what's going on, what you're doing, what your plans are." She rested her head against his chest again as he gently caressed her shoulders. "I've been in such a state of turmoil and I'm so confused."

His voice was soft. "I know and I'm sorry. I didn't mean for things to upset you. It's just that my plans formulated so quickly, took shape so rapidly—everything was moving so fast. When I left Beverly Hills on a three-month odyssey I had no idea anything like this would happen. The last thing I expected was to stop here and have someone as incredible as you literally fall into my life."

He paused, trying to get his thoughts together in some kind of logical manner. "Things happened so fast after that. Suddenly my head was full of thoughts and plans, plans that required a lot of groundwork to bring them to fruition. I felt alive again—felt that life still had meaning, still held challenges. I had to make decisions and I had to make them quickly. Everything I've done, all the plans I've made for the future have been with you in mind."

"If you were making plans for the future that included me, don't you think you should have consulted me?"

He allowed a slight smile to curl the corners of his mouth and a sigh to escape his lips. "You've got me there. You're absolutely right." He kissed her tenderly on the forehead. "Am I too late?"

"I..." Her words were hesitant. "I don't know." She felt his arms tighten around her.

"Don't say that, Cassie. I love you and you love me—that's the bottom line. Everything else can be worked out, starting right now.'' He released her from his embrace, placed his hands on her shoulders and captured her in the magnetic pull of his gaze. ''The first order of business is for me to dispel any worries and concerns you have about anything and everything.'' He took her hand and led her over to the couch and sat down.

''Now, I'll start by telling you what I have planned. Feel free to interrupt me at any time if you have any questions.'' For the next two hours he explained to her everything that he had done, all the preparations he had made so that he would be able to make a smooth transition from Beverly Hills to the island.

He took her hand and stood, pulling her to her feet next to him. ''Come on, I'll give you a tour of my new office, then a tour of my boat.'' He gazed lovingly into her eyes. ''And then I have something for you.''

Cassie was almost in a daze. Her mind whirled at the expanse of Trent's plans. She was still having difficulty grasping the magnitude of what he was putting together. He opened the front door and escorted her out onto the porch. She immediately spotted Jake lurking around the back door of the restaurant, watching the house. She turned a questioning look toward Trent.

''Yes, we had a couple of quiet words in the bar before I came up to the house. I owe Jake and lots of other people an explanation.'' He stopped walking, his brow furrowed in momentary concentration. ''Now might be a good time. I'll take everyone on a tour of the construction and explain what it is. And by everyone I mean Anne, Charlene and Danny, too. They were trying to be very unobtrusive but obviously hanging around the kitchen when I walked through. If you and Mike feel comfortable about leaving the bar in the hands of a few trusted customers, I'm sure he'd like to check things out, too.''

It was quite a parade as Trent led the little group next door. After he had left the bar and gone up to Cassie's house everyone had descended on Jake, demanding some answers. Since Trent was back and obviously dressed for success, Jake had felt it was okay to go ahead and tell them who Trent was but even Jake did not realize the full scope of exactly who and what Trent represented.

Trent had asked that everyone gather in the restaurant, away from the bar customers. "I owe all of you an explanation of what's going on here. First of all, I'd like to confirm what you probably all know by now. I'm an attorney and, up until quite recently, conducted a very lucrative practice in Beverly Hills. The mysterious white boat from Marina Del Rey that seemed to capture everyone's interest is back and belongs to me.''

He had everyone's rapt attention as he continued. "Now for what you don't know. I am T.A.N. Inc., the new owner of the motel.'' An immediate buzz of surprise rose from those assembled as eyes widened in shock. "The construction currently going on serves two purposes. First, the motel is being upgraded and expanded. Second, I'm adding a small office complex to take care of my other business interests since this is now my corporate headquarters. Among those interests will be the operation of a legal aid office to serve the needs of the people here and on the neighboring islands.''

Trent showed the group around the construction and made sure everyone met Grace. He also introduced Chad. Anne, Charlene, Danny and Mike talked excitedly among themselves as they left the motel and went back to the restaurant. Jake stayed behind with Cassie and Trent, who had invited him to go with them on a tour of the boat.

Jake was very impressed with Trent's boat. "No wonder you were able to handle my fishing boat so expertly. If you handle this big thing all by yourself, my little boat must have seemed like child's play." Cassie had been very quiet the entire time, both at the motel and on the boat. Jake looked at her questioningly. "What do you think, Cassie? Real nice, isn't it?"

Cassie spoke softly and without emotion. "Yes, it's very nice." Trent was unable to hide his anxiety and concern. She had not uttered a dozen words since they had left her house. He had no idea what her state of mind was. He could not read what she was hiding.

Jake took her silence and Trent's anxiety-ridden face as his cue to leave. "Well, I've got some errands to take care of, so I guess I'll be running along."

Trent put his hands on Cassie's shoulders and guided her back inside the main cabin of the boat. "You haven't said much. What are you thinking?"

She collapsed into a chair, a quick look of despair darting across her face. "I don't know what to think."

He knelt on the floor next to her chair, taking her hand in his and looking into her eyes. "I love you, Cassie, and I'm very sorry for the pain I've caused you. I know this has been a lot all at once. Have I left anything out? Do you have any questions that I haven't answered? Is there anything you want to know?"

"I don't know, Trent, I just don't know. So many things..." The tears welled in her eyes. "So many secrets. I just don't know."

He cupped her face in his hands, his eyes searching her face then finally settling on her eyes. "I promise you, there will never be any secrets again—never. I love you, Cassie. Without you, I have no life.''

Her gaze wandered around the cabin, as if actually taking it in for the first time. The past few hours had been mind-boggling—so many new things, so much to think about. ''Where does this leave us, Trent? You're now my new landlord. I make lease payments to you each month. Why do you have a drawing showing my restaurant as part of your motel? What is our relationship?'' A sob caught in her throat. ''And when will you decide this is tedious and it's time for you to move on again?''

''Move on? Is that what's bothering you?''

''Well...''

''Cassie, listen to me.'' He rose to his feet and pulled her up from the chair. Wrapping his arms around her, he held her head to his chest. His voice was calm, his tone loving. ''I've sold my half of a very lucrative Beverly Hills law firm to my partner, I've closed my house in Beverly Hills and put it up for sale, I've transferred all my financial dealings to Washington banks, I've formed a Washington corporation to operate my business interests, I've spent a lot of cash to buy out Bob Hampton and more to do extensive remodeling, all my personal belongings are being shipped here, I've moved two of my employees here and I'm even planning to take the Washington state bar exam so I can practice law in this state. Does that sound like someone who's just passing through?''

She slipped her arms around his waist and looked into the honesty of his blue eyes. Her words came out in a whisper. ''What about us?''

''Us? I want us to spend the rest of our lives together, that's what about us.'' He kissed her tenderly on the forehead then brushed his lips against hers. ''The reason

I had an artist's rendering showing the front of the restaurant and the motel as being connected was because it seemed like the logical thing for us to do with the two businesses after we were married.''

Her eyes widened. ''Married?''

''Of course, married. I love you and you love me. Where else could that possibly take us?'' He lowered his head and captured her mouth with a loving kiss. ''We'll apply for a marriage license first thing in the morning.'' He released her from his embrace, picked up his briefcase and opened it, removing a small velvet box. He took her hand and slipped the diamond ring on her finger. ''I love you very much, Cassie. Please do me the honor of becoming my wife.''

She looked at the ring, the brilliant diamond sparkling in a gold setting. She looked up into the honest love emanating from his blue eyes, then back at the ring. Her heart felt lighter than it ever had before as her love for him soared within her being. Tears of joy brimmed her eyes. ''I love you, Trent.''

Before anything else happened, he took a moment to remove a legal document from his briefcase. He handed the document to her. ''This is a prewedding present.''

Cassie looked at him questioningly, then looked at the document. She read it slowly and carefully. Tears welled in her eyes, her being filled to overflowing with the love she felt for him. ''Trent? Is this what I think it is?''

''If you think it's the deed to the land your restaurant and house sit on, then you're right. That's exactly what it is. I don't want there to be any doubts, concerns or fears on your part about exactly where things stand legally.''

Married! The word repeated over and over in her mind, competing with the love that welled up within her.

Married, the two of them husband and wife. She had never been so happy as she was at that moment. She looked at the deed, then at the ring on her finger. She slipped her arms around him, her voice soft and loving, yet with just a hint of a teasing quality. "Is this your idea of how to sweet-talk a girl into marrying you?"

He picked her up in his arms and whispered in her ear. "Have you ever made mad, passionate love on a boat?"

"That sounds more like a proposition than a proposal."

"It's both."

"I accept your proposal—" she smiled seductively as he carried her toward the bed "—and your proposition."

*   *   *   *   *

Silhouette Books has done it again!

Opening night in October has never been as exciting! Come watch as the curtain rises and romance flourishes when the stars of tomorrow make their debuts today!

Revel in Jodi O'Donnell's STILL SWEET ON HIM—
Silhouette Romance #969
...as Callie Farrell's renovation of the family homestead leads her straight into the arms of teenage crush Drew Barnett!

Tingle with Carol Devine's BEAUTY AND THE BEASTMASTER—
Silhouette Desire #816
...as legal eagle Amanda Tarkington is carried off by wrestler Bram Masterson!

Thrill to Elyn Day's A BED OF ROSES—
Silhouette Special Edition #846
...as Dana Whitaker's body and soul are healed by sexy physical therapist Michael Gordon!

Believe when Kylie Brant's McLAIN'S LAW —
Silhouette Intimate Moments #528
...takes you into detective Connor McLain's life as he falls for psychic—and suspect—Michele Easton!

Catch the classics of tomorrow—*premiering* today—
only from ♥ *Silhouette*

SILHOUETTE® Desire

OUTER BANKS

KEEGAN'S HUNT
by Dixie Browning

In November, Silhouette Desire has something very special for you—KEEGAN'S HUNT by Dixie Browning, Book One of her wonderful new series, *Outer Banks*.

In KEEGAN'S HUNT, infuriating yet irresistibly sexy ex-military man Richmond Keegan lands on Coronoke Island and immediately drives single mother Maudie Winters crazy...with desire!

Don't miss KEEGAN'S HUNT (#820) by Dixie Browning— only from Sihouette Desire.

SDDB1

And now for something completely different from Silhouette....

Every once in a while, Silhouette brings you a book that is truly unique and innovative, taking you into the world of paranormal happenings. And now these stories will carry our special "Spellbound" flash, letting you know that you're in for a truly exciting reading experience!

In October, look for *McLain's Law* (IM #528) by Kylie Brant

Lieutenant Detective Connor McLain believes only in what he can see—until Michele Easton's haunting visions help him solve a case...and her love opens his heart!

McLain's Law is also the Intimate Moments "Premiere" title, introducing you to a debut author, sure to be the star of tomorrow!

Available in October...only from Silhouette Intimate Moments

TAKE A WALK ON THE
DARK SIDE OF LOVE WITH

October is the shivery season, when chill winds blow and shadows walk the night. Come along with us into a haunting world where love and danger go hand in hand, where passions will thrill you and dangers will chill you. Silhouette's second annual collection from the dark side of love brings you three perfectly haunting tales from three of our most bewitching authors:

Kathleen Korbel
Carla Cassidy
Lori Herter

Haunting a store near you this October.

Only from 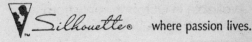 *Silhouette®* where passion lives.